INDEPENDENT
LEGIONS
PUBLISHING

THE CARP-FACED BOY AND OTHER TALES

by Thersa Matsuura

ISBN: 978-88-99569-37-2

1° edition paperback February 2017
Introduction by Gene O'Neill
Editing: Jodi Renée Lester
Cover Art: Daniele Serra

DEDICATION

For Mom and Dad,

Mom, whose generous and cheerful heart taught me to be open to life, cherish people, and when something knocks me down, to bounce back with vigor. You taught me kindness and love.

Dad, who taught me never to take anything at face value, to always ask why and how and what makes this thing/situation/person tick. From you, I learned to be questioning and curious.

SUMMARY

* "The Spider Sweeper"
    previously published in *Black Static* 41 (July-August 2014)

* "The Carp-Faced Boy"
    previously published in *The Beauty of Death* (2016)

Thersa Matsuura

The Carp-Faced Boy

and Other Tales

INTRODUCTION

Some Interesting Ways to Divide Horror
by Gene O'Neill

In discussions of the structure of horror, it is often defined by way of two extreme ends of a continuum. Let's take a look at three of the most popular or colorful divisions.

Karl Edward Wagner was a writer that dark fiction lost too early, passed away as a relatively young man. In addition to being an excellent writer of a wide range of fiction, including horror and sword and sorcery, he was a publisher and an editor of distinction. For a number of years he edited DAW Books' Best Horror series. Somewhere in one of those introductions, Karl made his colorful division of horror. He said that sometimes it was detached, quiet, and emotionally calm as if the characters were victims of a sniper, shooting so far in the distance his weapon made little sound. But at the other end of the continuum was a killer kicking in a door and blasting away with a shotgun. And even though Karl selected stories across the continuum for his Best series, he didn't say much about mixing the two extremes.

Of course academics have long divided horror fiction into two distinct categories, psychological or supernatural stories. They mean stories either have supernatural explanations—there are ghosts, vampires, werewolves, or otherworldly fantastic creatures scaring us. In these kinds of classic tales, events are normally external and do not usually conclude well for the protagonists. *Dracula* and *Frankenstein* come readily to mind. But in a story with a psychological explanation, significant events are mostly internal, seen from the point of view of the protagonist—he/she may be mentally unstable or deteriorating mentally before our eyes. A good example of this type of fiction is Charlotte Perkins Gilman's "The Yellow Wallpaper." Yes, and there are many stories that tread a thin line between both extremes. The exceptional story often leaves the explanation—psychological or supernatural—up to the reader. The great novella by Henry James *The Turn of the Screw* is usually considered a ghost story, but it can also be considered to have a psychological explanation—the governess perhaps mentally unstable.

When I was breaking into markets in the early-mid '80s, there were two distinct camps of horror fiction roughly similar to, but not exactly like, the academic division. There were dark fantasy and splatterpunk stories at the extreme ends. Dark fantasy, I believe, was a term Charles Grant used to guide writers in what he wanted for his Shadows anthology series. The stories were usually psychological in structure. But, occasionally, if there were a supernatural element, it was introduced in a *quiet* manner. Very little or no graphic violence. A Shadows story was more unsettling to the reader than terrifying. On the other hand a splatterpunk story was at the opposite end of the spectrum, lots of graphic violence, the blood and gore intended to have a terrifying effect. Skipp and Spector were early practitioners of this kind of tale. Of course good writers often practiced both extremes; and the best writers combined extremes in the same story, these stories often appearing in the Best of Horror anthologies.

And we come to Thersa Matsuura's very fine collection, *The Carp-Faced Boy and Other Tales.* As one might expect from the author's last name and title, the stories in the collection are heavily informed by Japanese culture, village architecture, superstitions, characterization, and even to some degree syntax. (Ms. Matsuura is actually an American who has lived in a Japanese village for many years). Still, to an American reader the stories have a slightly foreign *feel.* Technically, the writing is precise— the right verb chosen, eliminating the need for excessive use of adjectives or adverbs. More with less. The strongest aspect of all the stories is in the superior plotting, resulting in jolting surprises for the reader along the way. Even though the ten tales are varied in subject matter and tone—they range from a very odd alien story to the shortest one about a punk rock band—I think the tales that appear most traditional with an almost Japanese legend feel are my favorites.

They are also the stories that combine the quiet development of a psychological/dark fantasy explanation through the bulk of the story, but end with just a bit of supernatural/splatterpunk sensibility. I'll give examples from three favorite stories, without giving too much of the endings away, I hope.

"The Spider Sweeper" is about a gentle man living in a monastery who carefully sweeps up day spiders without damaging them—in fact he is called Kumo-harai, which in Japanese means *spider sweeper.* He reminds one of the Jainism religious sect of India who revere all life so much that they sweep in front of their path to ensure that tiny insects are not crushed and harmed. The bulk of "The Spider Sweeper" is essentially a psychological quiet love story between the common-man spider sweeper and a mysterious stranger, who revisits in a different form mid-story. But a bit of splatterpunk terror is introduced at the very end that shocks, but definitely makes the story result in a satisfying conclusion.

The title story, "The Carp-Faced Boy," is about a grumpy, reclusive grandfather, who nevertheless is kind to a horse that has carried his daughter and grandson for a visit to his rural village. We are introduced to the internal life of the grandfather and soon realize the old man may be suffering from a kind of demented paranoia directed at his grandson, whom the grandfather often describes in a very unflattering manner. So, the heart of the tale is psychological and quiet. But the story concludes in the grandest of splatterpunk manners indeed.

"Pinwheels and Spider Lilies," concerns another common man, actually kind of a loser. Akito has lost his job, his wife, and his daughter. But we learn he is grateful for the very little that life brings him. A supernatural element is introduced early in the form of a mountain witch, who demands a number of trades with Akito. But the transactions are not too terrifying or demanding, the story moves along in the quiet dark fantasy manner. Akito even regains first his daughter, and then his wife. But as we might guess, all does not end well for our protagonist.

I have Thersa Matsuura's name underlined on the side of my fridge. I will watch for her byline. As I'm sure, you, the reader of this collection will, too.

--Gene O'Neill, *Lethal Birds* and The Cal Wild Chronicles

THERSA MATSUURA

THE SPIDER SWEEPER

Kumo-harai balanced a fat-bellied spider on the end of an old, twiggy broom. He was hurrying to reach the persimmon tree before the creature leapt to the ground and scrambled away. Morning spiders were always taken to the same tree and carefully placed in its craggy branches. Everyone knew that they were good luck and should never be harmed. Kumo-harai could boast—if he were the type of man to do such a thing—that in his three years of working at the temple he had never killed or injured a single morning spider.

His kindheartedness, though, embraced even the night spiders, which were all thieves and should be crushed beneath a tightly woven sandal. These creatures he feared. Placing his palms together as he saw the monks do every day, he bowed, recited some pieces of the Heart Sutra he'd managed to memorize, and left the night spiders entirely alone. It had never occurred to the young man that they could possibly be the same exact creature.

It was early and he was depositing a green and yellow harlot spider on a low branch the first time he heard the voice behind his ear.

"Kumo-harai."

It was his lover who had been gone for six days. Excitement swelled in his chest and he spun around. But there was no one there, only a wet, early morning mist settling into the leafy ground and beyond that the old wooden temple, its paper doors pushed open. He could see the monks filing quietly into the main hall for meditation. A bronze bell rang in low waves across the graveyard; and Kumo-harai's heart broke for the second time.

"Kumo-harai," the voice whispered again.

Kumo-harai. The Spider Sweeper. It wasn't his real name, but it was what everyone called him, ever since the monks of the Yamaoku Temple had taken him in. It was his job.

He was just one of too-many children, a boy who didn't work particularly hard at anything, who would rather stare at a cloudless sky half the day than mend the broken *geta* of a beautiful woman. But still he was attractive enough for the go-betweens in town to seek out his parents and attempt to arrange marriages for him. But no matter how much status or money the offering family had, Kumo-harai—much to his parents' shame—always fled their requests.

The young man was eventually taken to the local soothsayer who deemed him one of those poor souls who were bound to loneliness their entire lives. He would need more than he would ever give, she explained. And over time this would consume all of the family's fortune and luck. She suggested he be sent away, that the lessons he needed to learn were under some other roof. His parents agreed. It was only the monks who were able to find the work he could do and the quiet that he desired.

"Kumo-harai."

It was then he saw in the thin blue predawn light a tall handsome man with his sedge *sandogasa* hat thrown back and his long hair loose around his shoulders, his hands open and empty by his sides. It was Jin. Kumo-harai felt an immediate rush of affection well and then crash into clammy terror. The fog shifted, the vision faded, and the young man collapsed on the ground and wept until the head abbot found him on his way to the toilet half a day later.

The head abbot was a serious man with small foxlike eyes that were sunk too far apart on his face. This might have been handsome had he a strong nose and mouth. But he didn't. His nose was the shape of a sticky rice ball rolled by a pair of tiny hands, his mouth the color of an earthworm and perpetually downturned. When he smiled—which wasn't often—he showed his bad, almost pointy teeth. Still he was a man of great wisdom and patience, whom many of the townspeople came to for consolation and advice. Do not be deceived by appearances was one of his more frequent sermons.

Kumo-harai buried his face in the abbot's old silk robes, scratching his cheek on the rough-edged holes burned into the fabric by the daily spitting fire of the purification ceremony. He was embarrassed at his emotions and his lack of control, but the sobbing wouldn't cease. The abbot was a magnanimous man and didn't ridicule him or spout the Buddha's teachings of non-attachment. He merely held the young man close to his chest, rocking him and waiting for his explanation.

When he was able, Kumo-harai described what he'd seen and heard. The abbot nodded but said nothing. Later that day a pair of traveling monks arrived. They were given a meal and a blessing and sent right back out to see if they could learn something to put their spider sweeper's fears aside.

The next day the vision returned. It strode across the graveyard and disappeared near the thick-walled storehouse where the monks kept their pickled vegetables and rice. Kumo-harai cried out, disturbing the morning's meditation, but by the time the abbot arrived the ghost had vanished. Kumo-harai insisted on being taken to the soothsayer. Maybe she'd have an answer.

The abbot steadfastly refused, stating that she was a charlatan preying off of people's fears. But after the third day when the apparition, Jin, returned again with the morning mist and marched across the yard and into the storehouse, Kumo-harai abandoned his work and went alone to the woman who seemed to know truth much more than the monks.

"Your relationship...," she started.

"We're friends. We became friends when he visited the temple one month ago."

"Friends," she repeated, rattling a bamboo cup full of long sticks.

"It's like I've met him before. I would say I know him better than I know any of my brothers or sisters," Kumo-harai paused. "And he knows me."

"This is evidenced by his visits," the bent and warted woman said. "Sometimes strong emotions can cause a person's spirit to leave their body. Emotions of hate, jealousy..." The woman squinted at the fidgeting young man. "Love," she continued slowly as if judging his reaction.

"So it's not a ghost I'm seeing?" Kumo-harai asked. "Just his spirit missing me?"

"You say the vision calls out to you and walks to the storehouse?" the old woman asked in response.

"Yes."

"Why the storehouse?" She gave the sticks one more shake and then scattered them across the floor.

Kumo-harai was rinsing off his broom in the river when the traveling mendicant first arrived. He was darkly tanned, lean and long-muscled. He was filthy. Kumo-harai crouched by a hydrangea bush and picked up a stick, quietly pretending to remove the more obstinate threads of web buried deep in the bristles of the broom. He observed the stranger from the corner of his eye.

The stranger placed his walking stick and pack on a rock. He removed his leggings and sandals and stripped down to his *shitaobi*. Untying his cone-shaped hat, he used it to cover his belongings. Finally, he removed a small length of twine from his hair before he climbed a boulder and plunged head first into the icy water. Kumo-harai watched him swim, his own hands temporarily forgetting his made-up task.

After some time the man returned to the shallow bank and stood, his long black hair falling down to the small of his back. He rubbed his body and face with handfuls of soft sand until the grime and dust that had accumulated from his travels disappeared and his skin shone red. He cupped his hands and drank deeply from the river.

"You, over there!" the stranger called, turning to face Kumo-harai. He was beautiful. "This is the best tasting water I've had since Joanji in Shima. There must be magic in these mountains."

Kumo-harai rose, took a step, and stumbled. He didn't think he'd been seen. Had the stranger known he'd been watching the whole time? Maybe he was talking to someone else. Kumo-harai looked over both shoulders. The dark man laughed.

"Is that your temple up there?" He pointed to the silver-tiled roof visible through the trees.

Kumo-harai shouldered his broom and nodded.

"You don't talk, do you?"

As it turned out Kumo-harai did talk. He just wasn't used to

20

being talked to. The monks only spoke when something needed conveying. And other than the tofu seller who delivered the morning meal at dawn, there was really no one except the birds and the insects and the murmuring spirits that rattled the wooden grave tablets to converse with.

Before the day ended in purple and blue, Kumo-harai learned the mendicant was called Jin, the son of a paper maker up north in Echigo. Five years ago an outbreak of smallpox ravaged his town and he lost his entire family. Heartbroken he renounced his trade and possessions and set out to travel down Japan visiting all of the sixty-six holy sites.

When Kumo-harai asked what he was searching for, Jin said he didn't know, that maybe he was running from something or toward something, but the real answer was probably that he was simply afraid. Kumo-harai fell asleep that night admiring deeply this stranger and wondering why his own kind of fear didn't encourage movement but left him too scared to do anything at all.

The next day Kumo-harai discovered they were the same age, although Jin looked much older with his sunburned and lined face and the slight limp he'd taken on from his years of traveling. But it wasn't just that, there was a hushed energy about him that suggested deep thought or a long-lived life. Kumo-harai couldn't help but address him in the overly polite language he usually spoke only to the abbot of the temple.

At first the townspeople were wary of the dark-skinned stranger. Even the monks while allowing him to stay—as they

21

must any itinerant disciple of the Buddha—were watchful. And so for fifteen days Jin spent all of his time with Kumo-harai helping him with his many chores. They replaced the oil in the *andon* lanterns, raked the embers from under the bath, and pulled kudzu from the stone stairs of the temple. And every morning they woke before dawn and carefully swept away the spiders from the rafters and the gravestones and set them gently on the shivering limbs of the old persimmon tree.

There was a familiarity with Jin that Kumo-harai had never felt before, something comfortable. Days passed much more quickly than they ever had before, and yet at night, tossing on a threadbare futon, there were so many things to remember that the young man found himself refusing sleep just to reexamine each memory one by one.

There was the dark stranger and there were his stories. Jin would recount his travels, teaching Kumo-harai folk tales and superstitions from as far away as Hizen and Tosa. During the day on trips to and from the river, two slatted barrels across their shoulders, he'd tell him funny and curious customs.

"In Kyushu they call spiders *kobu* instead of *kumo*," he explained one day as they rested for a while with their backs pressed against a leaning gravestone. Jin held a tiny sunset-red spider on the back of his hand.

"*Kobu*," Kumo-harai repeated, liking the silly sound of the dialect.

"The night spiders are referred to as *yoru kobu* instead of *yoru kumo*." Jin blew lightly on the insect and it hopped onto a bent

22

strand of grass. He then crossed both arms over his knees, rested his chin on his forearms and waited.

Kumo-harai smiled, finally understanding the play on words.

"It sounds like *yorokobu,* happiness," Kumo-harai said. "So night spiders are good luck there?"

"The more I travel the more I realize all things, even your perception of things, are only a matter of the words ascribed," Jin said. "Or so it seems." He looked Kumo-harai in the eyes for a long time. "People would be better off being quiet. Like you."

Later in the day Jin's accounts would invariably turn to the macabre, eerie folklore of beautiful women with greedy mouths concealed in the backs of their heads, or impossibly thin, hungry ghosts that swilled their long tongues into unattended oil lamps. He even told of giant spiders that hid in the forest only venturing out occasionally to crack the skulls of unsuspecting victims and feast on the soft of their brains.

When it was finally judged that Jin wasn't a wandering bandit, that he was indeed full of fascinating stories and news from all over Japan, the townspeople began to come around. And soon it wasn't just Kumo-harai who loved the dark stranger named Jin.

Women gathered to learn remedies for skin ailments and weak stomachs; men came to ask about the state of certain territories, the lords who reigned there, and the outcome of various battling clans. Even the children tugged at the man's robes, begging a new game or song. Some days he sat for hours in empty rice fields teaching the little ones how to make whistles from the stems of dandelions.

One day while Jin and Kumo-harai were picking devil's tongue to dry for the abbot's tea, several young women approached. After much giggling, they asked him to describe the fabled Shimada chignon they'd heard so much about. One woman let down her hair and asked boldly if he thought he could show them how it was made. It was at that moment that Kumo-harai felt an emotion he'd never had before. He removed the basket from his hip and spent the rest of the day alone by the river. By nightfall he was no longer angry but terrified in a way he'd never been before.

The next day the two worked side by side as usual and Kumo-harai tried to pretend that nothing inside him had changed. But what was once comfortable was now awkward, and he could find nothing to talk about. Even Jin seemed to be more distant than usual. After the evening meal, Jin built a small fire behind the graveyard to keep off the chill and used his walking stick to knock the branches of the chestnut tree. The two gathered and roasted the prickly treats in silence.

"Those are the temples you've visited," Kumo-harai said, pointing to characters burned into the thick staff. There were stylized characters nearly impossible to read all up and down the hard wood.

"All of them so far," Jin said, turning it in his hands to show his friend. "I've still got five more stops."

"Five more," Kumo-harai repeated, he leaned over and ran his finger down the impressions until he reached the last one. Yamaoku Temple. His temple. It was a small stamp. They weren't one of the sixty-six holy sites. They hardly ever had traveling monks visit; most carried on until they reached the city.

Jin kicked up a sharp rock and examined it. He took the stick and under the last stamp began to carve something in the empty space.

Kumo-harai used the end of his broom to poke the fire.

"Your next stop is Mishima," Kumo-harai said.

"Yes."

Kumo-harai turned and faced his friend. Nights were coming more quickly and already the air was a rich indigo. Jin's profile was lit orange and red from the fire. Even his black hair, pulled away from his face and tied back, looked as if it had been splashed with paint or sunlight. He stopped carving and threw the rock aside. He blew on the wood.

"You have to leave," Kumo-harai said. It wasn't a question.

"Yes," Jin answered. "But I'll return before autumn next year."

"That's a long time."

"Not so long." Jin gazed into the darkening forest. The moon, not quite full, was still low and large rising over the tree line. The night insects chirred. "I'll be back in time for spider season. I'll be here to help."

Kumo-harai smiled. From inside the temple the last bell of the evening tolled, slow silver reverberations washing over them. The monks could be heard shuffling barefoot across the straw-matted floors to their rooms. Their prayers were finished for the day. Jin handed Kumo-harai his walking stick turning it so he could see the newly made inscription.

Kumo-harai. He'd carved his name.

"You're the gentlest soul I've ever met," Jin said. "Someone who greets the birds by the names he's given them, who whispers appreciation to bath water before he throws it out, and who sees the world as it should be, not as it is." Jin held out his hands and examined them in the firelight. They were old man's hands. "You made me battle myself. You confused me." He finally turned to meet Kumo-harai's stare. "And I could very well end my journey here. Stay here. Forever."

Kumo-harai felt his breath hitch in his chest. He wanted to cry out. The bell's ringing faded, split, and then shattered into a beautiful chorus of crickets erupting from the forest. The sound crested the mountains and fell away; it went on and on. It was just for them.

The last paper door in the temple slid shut across its wooden track. Jin reached out and took Kumo-harai's hand. He stood and led him to the grassy patch behind the storage house where there the moonlight fell and the night-blooming jasmine ran up the back of the stone building.

Jin was still asleep when Kumo-harai left to fetch water and start the morning fires. When he returned he found the graveyard wet with morning dew and a heavy mist. The same as it was every day but different. The spiders had been busy and even in the faint morning light their webs glistened in long jewel-lined threads from gravestone to gravestone. Standing near a mossy lantern was Jin. He was dressed in his traveling clothes. Kumo-harai felt the strength leave his legs, but the dark man was there to hold him up and kiss him one last time hard on the mouth.

Afterward, Jin announced his departure and the abbot hastily arranged for a pilgrimage ceremony to be performed.

The monks lit a large fire and fed it with damp grasses and handfuls of fragrant herbs. A constant rhythm was beaten on *taiko* drums, bells were rung, and deep-voiced trance-inducing tones were chanted. Jin knelt before the abbot, head bowed, receiving the blessing. Before long the townspeople were making their way up the mountain to wish their new friend a safe journey. Kumo-harai hid in the plumes of cedar- and sage-scented smoke, allowing them to sting and water his eyes.

When the ceremony ended, Jin was presented with a bundle of food and fresh water for his journey. The children looped several dandelion necklaces around his neck and played little tunes on the stems. Kumo-harai remained apart from the crowd. He wanted to run to him, to beg him to stay. Jin said goodbye to each person in turn. When he was finished he went to Kumo-harai.

"I forgot to return this," Jin said, pressing something into the palm of his hand. Kumo-harai squeezed the object tightly, and with his other hand held Jin's wrist.

"Thank you," he said, bowing low.

Jin returned the bow and speaking in a low voice said, "If I don't leave now I'll never go. It was a promise I made on my parents' grave, my sisters' grave. I have to—"

"I know," Kumo-harai said, slipping his hand up Jin's sleeve, holding his forearm for a long moment before he pulled away.

While Jin was putting on his sedge hat and tying it around his chin, Kumo-harai opened his palm to find a tiny Buddha carved out of pink coral. He knew its story. It had belonged to Jin's mother.

Kumo-harai, thinking he'd see him again, watched the broad back of his lover walk away.

Kumo-harai waited as the soothsayer examined the sticks on the straw-matted floor.

"Yes, yes, that's what it is," she said. "His spirit is visiting you."

Kumo-harai was almost ready to believe her prediction when one of the monks from the temple flung open the door and prostrated himself on the dirt floor.

"The abbot said I'd find you here," he said. He was out of breath. "I have news."

Kumo-harai made his hands into fists and closed his eyes.

"There were bandits on the road," the monk said. "Jin was alone." The young monk couldn't even look Kumo-harai in the eyes. "He was murdered."

"But he was a traveling mendicant," Kumo-harai said. "He had nothing of value..."

He reached up to touch the collar of his robe, running his finger along the outline of the small Buddha he'd sewn there three nights ago. He wondered, if Jin had not given it to him, could he have used it to buy his own life?

When Kumo-harai woke the next morning, he could hardly remember being carried back to the temple and laid in his drafty room, a wooden pillow pushed up under his neck, a futon pulled to his chest. He was alone.

Down the hallway he could hear chanting and drumming and the crackle of the morning fire. A very faint light came from behind the paper *shoji*. He had overslept and someone had performed his morning chores for him. He hurried into the graveyard. It was the fourth morning since the ghost first appeared and Kumo-harai prayed he was not too late to see him again.

"Kumo-harai."

The ghost was waiting. It turned its back and strode across the yard toward the storehouse, the first and last place they'd been together.

This time Kumo-harai followed his lover, wiping away tears with the back of his long sleeve until he reached the heavy storehouse door. Collapsing against the splintering wood he wept.

"Kumo-harai," the voice was coming from inside of the building. He pushed himself up and pulled at the handle. The door opened.

It was dark inside, the morning sun lighting only a long rectangle on the clay floor. The smell of earth and the sour odor of vinegared daikon filled Kumo-harai's head. He stepped inside. He squinted trying to find Jin's ghost in the dark corners of the room. But it had vanished again.

"What are you doing there?!"

Kumo-harai jumped. He hadn't heard anyone approaching.

"I..."

"Did you see him again?" The abbot opened up his arms and Kumo-harai went to him.

It was there in that embrace, the abbot gently leading the young man from the storehouse, that Kumo-harai turned for one last glance into the room and saw what he was meant to see.

There, hastily shoved into a corner, was a bundle of clothes. Traveling clothes, a large cone-shaped hat ripped nearly in half, and a traveling staff. These were not the style of clothes the monks used when they did their own travels. These were layman's clothes, mendicant's clothes. Kumo-harai pushed himself free of the abbot and ran over to the pile. He buried his face in them and knew. These were Jin's belongings. And they were covered in blood.

With the sun in his eyes he looked back up at the abbot. "How did you get these?" For a moment Kumo-harai still believed that bandits had killed his lover.

The fox-eyed man, a large black figure in the doorway, folded his arms across his chest and said nothing.

"You did this?" Kumo-harai held the walking stick, the top splintered. Jin had put up a fight. But who knows how many were sent after him. "There were no bandits. It was you?"

Still the monk stood silent.

"Why? He had nothing of value. He was good man," Kumo-harai, his voice cracking with grief, realizing just now this wasn't about riches. "He'd gone. He was already gone."

"He was a risk," the older man said.

"What do you—"

"I had him followed into the city. Just to be sure," the abbot said.

Kumo-harai rubbed his thumb along the last carving in the staff; the one Jin had made that night by the fire—his name. He pushed himself up and approached the abbot. He stopped an arm's length away. "Why?"

"You were mine. You were always meant to be mine," the abbot said, looking straight into the young man's eyes. "Jin should have stayed gone."

"Stayed gone?" Kumo-harai thought he was going to be sick. "You mean he was coming back?" He tightened his grip on the walking stick.

"Yes."

"For me?"

"Yes." The abbot spit on the floor, raised his mashed dumpling nose in contempt.

The edges of Kumo-harai's vision disappeared in smudged ink. He saw nothing but the monster in front of him. He raised the stick and screamed. The abbot backed out into the graveyard tripping on his robes. Kumo-harai waited for him to stand before he advanced again.

To his right the temple stood, doors pushed open. Lines of straight-backed monks droned sutras and sleepy prayers. The hollow wooden drum clacked a steady beat. A golden bell. The men were used to the occasional day when the head monk slept in or had business elsewhere. They were single-minded in their meditations or resolute in their betrayal—either way, not a single man lifted his eyes to witness the crying out and pleading of their master going on below.

The last vision Kumo-harai ever saw of Jin was over the abbot's shoulder. He was standing under the persimmon tree, bare-chested and smiling.

Kumo-harai knew exactly what he needed to do. Step by step, the jagged end of the walking stick thrust into the fat of the old man's throat, he led the abbot through the graveyard down to the tree line until he had his back pressed against the twisted trunk of the persimmon tree. The old monk tried to make excuses, he wept. But Kumo-harai wasn't swayed. And for the first time he could remember, he wasn't afraid.

"If you kill me, you'll forever suffer in one of Buddha's hells, roasting over a sulfur fire, your belly split and boiling," the abbot warned, shaking his fist, trying to look intimidating. "You'll never be with Jin again."

"Oh, you will not die by my hand," Kumo-harai said. "I have no desire to meet you in hell."

A brief expression of hope passed across the fox-eyed man's face. He smiled an awful, sharp-toothed smile. He ran one hand over his shaven head and clucked his tongue. Such a shaming

32

sound. Such a confident sound. Kumo-harai would enjoy putting an end to that.

He raised Jin's staff above his head and brought it down on the branches overhead. The tree trembled, raining down morning dew, dying leaves, and spiders. Hundreds and hundreds of spiders. Spiders in all shapes and sizes. Some dropped on the abbot's saffron robes, finding purchase and scuttling into folds or down his neckline, while others landed on the ground only to disappear under the man's yellow hem, scurrying up the abbot's fat legs. While the old man was busy yelping and slapping them away, he didn't notice the others, the ones that swung down on delicate threads. The ones that lowered themselves slowly, intentionally. He screamed, flailed. He stomped and howled.

And Kumo-harai laughed and laughed as he beat the tree; for a few minutes anyway. That is until something made him stop.

Even the abbot ceased his thrashing when he saw Kumo-harai's face, saw him gazing over his shoulder, beyond the persimmon tree, deeper into the forest. Eyes wide and mouth ajar.

"Wha-what is it?" the old monk asked. But he didn't turn. He watched as Kumo-harai dropped the walking stick and then clutched at the collar of his robe, kissing it and whispering a prayer. The young man stumbled backward. He saw what was coming.

But the abbot was frozen with fear, couldn't move. Could probably not even guess what the younger man saw. He might have heard the sound of something horrible and hungry moving along the leafy forest floor, the snap and splinter of tree limbs as it approached. A heavy moldy woof of its breath. But the old monk had never been there to listen to Jin's stories. His imagination couldn't possibly allow the idea that the crack of a small tree being bent in half was some enormous beast coming to feed. A monster picking its way closer and closer on eight grotesque legs, dozens of eyes glassy and wild. No, the abbot couldn't imagine that or even this: that a moment later—an instant after he felt the fiery heat of the beast—there might be another echoing crack to fill his ears. And this time it wouldn't be a tree or a branch but the very peculiar and satisfying sound made by a jealous man's head being opened and cleaned of the treasure inside.

SASA'S ROUGED CHEEKS, SASA'S REDDENED LIPS

"Sasa dear, don't you think you're making a mistake?" Mother asked, dipping two fingers into a bowl of warm rapeseed oil and massaging it into the knotty horns that protruded from the girl's hairline. Horns that weren't even as long as her pinky yet. Hadn't even grown sharp.

"Not in the least." Sasa's toothy grin said it all.

Mother felt a weary sigh build in her chest, a sprig of anger tickled her tongue. Bitter. Delicious. This was a battle she was losing, but she had to try.

"You realize your brothers are furious?" Mother wiped her hands on a torn shred of cloth and reached for another ceramic bowl. "And if your father were here—"

35

"I don't care what they think," Sasa interrupted. "They don't know him. They're just jealous."

Jealous, Mother thought. Possessive. Cautious. Wise. These were better words.

She cupped her daughter's head in her hands and tilted it up. With the balls of her thumbs she slowly rubbed the blood red of crushed safflowers into the girl's high-muscled cheeks.

"*Okaasan*," Sasa's tone lightened. "He's the one. Without a doubt. Him."

The anger shot down the older woman's throat and filled her stomach. Her hands wanted to squeeze, wanted to shake, wanted to snap. You'll lose her forever if you aren't careful, Mother thought. There's always the chance she'll return. She remembered her own youthful rebellion. The regret.

"He's a man, Sasa. He's soft and useless and he's turned you soft, too." Mother ran her vermillion-dyed thumbs over the girl's lips and then across her sharp-set teeth and gums. "He'll betray you the first chance he gets."

"He will not. And what's wrong with soft anyway?" Sasa pushed herself away. She snatched the folded *yukata* off the floor and thrust her arms into the sleeves. "I can do this myself."

But she couldn't. Mother attempted a smile and then motioned for her daughter to come back to her. A pause and Sasa came. She was weak.

The two were silent as Mother tucked and tied the long length of cloth, a pattern of blossom-pink butterflies flittering across a beryl-colored night. Left over right. A hem that falls straight, barely brushing the tops of her feet. A tug at each shoulder and a last aligning of the neckline curving down the front of Sasa's broad frame. Mother, satisfied with her work, next began to wrap a wide obi of darker blue around and around her daughter's waist. She pulled it until it pinched and then twisted it into a complicated bow at the small of the girl's back.

"Was this his idea?" Mother asked, referring to the summer garment.

"This? No, this is a surprise," Sasa said. She held out her arms and waggled the dangling sleeves. Her giddy mood had returned. She started spinning on the balls of her feet.

Ludicrous, like a human on too much spoiled rice drink.

Today was the last day of Obon, the Festival for the Dead. The sun had set an hour ago, and all the townspeople would be gathered to celebrate and send their long-deceased ancestors back to the Other Side.

"Okaasan, he doesn't care what I look like," Sasa said. "It's true."

Oh, but he does, the older woman thought. Oh, but he will.

Mother nodded and began to work on her daughter's unruly hair. Running sweet camellia oil through the tangled black strands, her crone's hands lifted, smoothed, gathered, and pinned. When she was done she added an ornament: a comb with a spray of fine golden wires, every one of them ending in a pea-sized bell. Sasa shook her head and a shimmer of music filled the room, an angelic chorus designed to cool the August heat and add lightness to the summer months.

Mother heard it differently. To her the tinkling sound was a warning. It chided and announced there was nothing she could do to stop the events of the day. The fight was lost.

"What does his family think?" Mother asked.

"He doesn't have a family. That's what's perfect. He lost them all last year to the God of Pox." Sasa spun again, clumsy on her bare feet. She wasn't beautiful and brutal like her brothers. She wasn't beautiful or brutal at all.

No family? Mother remembered the previous spring when the pox rode in on a northeasterly wind. It was a great heinous god that seeded the townspeople's lungs and then chewed great boils across their skin. It fed until its belly grew huge. Still, its appetite remained insatiable. It took hundreds, every single one it tortured until screaming, tortured until dead.

Heavy footfall entering the room knocked Mother from her thoughts. A presence like the sun on her back. Her eldest. Her dearest. More majestic and more cruel than her dead husband, he was getting harder and harder to control.

"She's not leaving." His voice made Sasa flinch and lower her head.

The girl's reaction to her brother spurred a flicker of a memory: Mother's own escape when she was about the same age. How difficult it had been.

The older woman ignored her favorite son and picked up the wooden *geta* shoes. She held them out to Sasa. After tonight she'd never see her daughter again. This she knew for sure.

38

"I don't suggest you wear these. They're uncomfortable," were her last words of advice.

Sasa took the shoes and put them on.

Mother caught the hazel-eyed gaze of her son and shook her head. No. Don't.

"Let her go," she said.

Outside the night sky exploded. Fireworks. The Obon festival had begun.

With tiny, tottering steps, geta threatening to splinter under her feet, Sasa skirted the town, the festival, and the crowds of hating people. She crept through the trees to the clearing her lover called home. A twig snapped and gave way, and her ankle threatened to turn at a bad angle.

Ridiculous shoes, Sasa thought, wondering why she'd even worn them in the first place. They slowed her down. She had to hurry. Choushichi was waiting. He'd been waiting since sundown.

She stumbled into the field to see him outlined by the fire at his feet. His body leaned heavy on the walking stick he gripped with both hands. She was about to call out when suddenly the raven-colored sky exploded into color again, a shower of crimson and gold fell in slow ribbons. A moment later the sound, a sickening punch in her stomach.

Choushichi didn't move and didn't look up either. There was something wrong. Had he changed his mind? Would he when he knew what she had to tell him? She kicked off the stupid shoes and raced across the meadow, her ornament singing in her hair.

"I made you wait," she said.

"But you came." Choushichi turned. His face was pockmarked; his half-smile, a sneer.

"Your mother let you leave." He sounded surprised.

"She did."

"Your brothers, too?"

In the firelight the creamy oyster milk of his eyes glittered. It always looked like he was about to cry. Choushichi was hideous. A monster. It was why the town had ostracized him and part of the reason Sasa had fallen in love.

"Yes, my brothers, too," she said.

"I hear bells, the rub of cloth." Choushichi leaned forward and squinted. Sometimes he pretended he could see. More than once Sasa wondered, had it been easier for him to lose his family than his sight? He didn't talk about them at all.

He touched one of her sleeves. "Hemp, and such a fine weave."

"Choushichi." Sasa took his hand in hers. The suffocating that had been building in her lungs frightened her. She'd never felt it before. Was it warning her to keep her secret? Was it love?

"There is something…" She placed the flat of his hand on top of the sash pulled tight around her belly. She pressed down. "This."

"Sasa?"

But they didn't get to say anything more. From the forest came distant shouts and the clumsy noise of men's feet trampling underbrush. Choushichi stepped back.

"They found out about us," he said. "They're coming."

"I know."

"What are we going to do?" he asked. "There are too many."

"I'll take care of it." To calm him she brought the hand that she hoped understood to her lips.

"It'll be okay," she said.

Choushichi shuddered as she rubbed the tips of his fingers across her teeth. Harder. The saltiness on her tongue, the way it warmed her throat. Nearly forgotten memories filled her head: the meaty tang and tenderness of human flesh and what little effort it took to tear it like an overripe peach's skin.

The men from the village broke the tree line. Shouts and curses. All of them driven savage by anger, hate. They spotted Sasa and her lover silhouetted against the dying fire. They came.

Sasa smiled. It was happening, what she missed most about the hunt, the fight, the kill. All around her the world became song. Her racing heart fell in time with the rhythmic thump-thump-thump of *taiko*-drums echoing off the distant summer festival. The glassy lilt of a dozen wooden flutes slithered around her waist, slipped between her legs. Tightening, tightening.

Sasa pushed Choushichi behind her. The men were almost on them. She filled her lungs and let the gamy scent of human sweat enrage her blood. Wait. Not yet. Not yet. Her vision widened.

Sharpened. She saw everything. She heard everything. She couldn't lose her mind yet. Not yet.

Sasa moaned at the pulsing down below and concentrated on the soothing odor of oiled rags burning, smoke, and the smell of grass and loam kicked up by the driving drumbeat of feet pounding earth. Closer. Not yet. She crouched ready to spring. Sasa hadn't killed in over a year.

"There they are!" barked the town's seer. The seer was a man who made his fortune by tossing yarrow sticks and pretending to comprehend the impossible-to-know future.

"Monsters! Abominations!" he goaded from the back of the mob.

Sasa understood the seer. He was like all weak men. He feared what he didn't understand. But being afraid was something he could never admit to himself or others. So he had to hate what he didn't understand, too. He had to hate it, and to prove he was strong, he had to destroy it.

Sasa waited until the first man was almost upon her. She lunged. The horde closed in. Arms raised, clubs swinging down, across, fists and blades. Sasa moved effortlessly between their blows, the easy way her claws caught fabric, found the skin underneath, and the satisfying splitting sensation of both as her enemy pulled away in a useless attempt at escape. The mounting pinch between her legs throbbing, throbbing.

More men rushed in. Sasa's head dizzied with the fetid stench of anger soured to fear. Intoxicating. She grabbed the next man and sunk her teeth into his flesh, flesh that yielded until it gave, releasing the sweet juice inside. Sasa sucked. She cried out loud. Discordant screams erupting around her as they fell one after the other.

Some men die noisily, howling like animals, so desperate to hold on to their lives; some men go in absolute silence, unaware even that they are dead. Her favorites, though, the men she almost pitied, were the ones who went sweetly, a futile prayer trapped in the popping spittle on their lips.

That's when Sasa saw him. She was almost surprised. Tomo, the wild boar hunter, little more than a child. Just yesterday she sat watching him from the shadows, that pouty mouth whispering apologies to the pigs he was about to slay. Only now the full lips were black lines, framing bared teeth. He sprang at her, shrieking.

It happened in an instant. Sasa's right hand flew up to grab the back of the boy's head. A second's hesitation. Regret? He was a little like her. He also didn't fit in. Sasa screamed and twisted his head hard. The snap she heard could have been one of the logs popping on the fire.

He dropped. Tomo the wild boar hunter, she thought, little more than a child. Sasa mumbled an apology and stepped over the boy's body, so much smaller in death.

Only the seer was left now, hanging back, heavy club cocked on his shoulder. In the quiet before his attack, the staccato dripping as the blood from her claws hit the wet chest of a body at her feet. It added a somber note to the end of the song.

"Monsters," he growled. "Both of you. You shouldn't be allowed to live."

With that the seer charged. Sasa spun, knocking the weapon from his hand. He never stood a chance. Like all weak men, he'd spent his entire life convincing others to do his work for him. He was useless. Sasa tore the material from his chest, the skin from his bones. She licked the dirty sweat from his bare shoulder and looked him in his panicked eyes to see if he had anything else he wanted to say.

The mounting pinch between her legs burned like fire now, cresting. She could hardly stand it. The seer whimpered and tried to scramble away. There was no need to draw it out. A back broken over her knee. The last man fell.

Finally the burning coil that had been tightening inside snapped, flooding her with heat and sending electricity up her middle and down her thighs. Sasa gasped, eyes rolled back in her head, she stumbled.

"We have to go," she said. Choushichi appeared from the shadows, unharmed.

"Yes," he stammered. There was an uncertainty in his voice she'd never heard before.

She reached out and took his hand, worried he'd withdraw, worried that he'd changed his mind. Was it all too much for him? The reason they had to escape, him witnessing who she used to be. But she wasn't like that anymore. She was changing. Did he understand that?

Her skin was slick with blood and cold. His was hot and dry. Would he be okay? They were all each other had. But more than that, she loved him.

"Let's go," he said and squeezed her hand, reassuring her. He wasn't afraid. Sasa felt light again, that hopeful human feeling that was new to her.

But it wasn't going to be that easy. She took one step and stopped. The wind had changed and with it came a pungent animal reek, familiar and dangerous. Dread. Not him, she thought. Not them. She imagined her brothers in the forest, crouching behind trees, clinging to the creaking limbs overhead. Fierce and unforgiving. She could almost hear them gnashing their teeth and hissing their disgust. They were waiting though. Why?

Sasa glanced down at the carnage around her, thankful it was hidden from Choushichi. She never wanted him to know how cruel and unfair the world really was.

Then she understood why her brothers hadn't attacked. Yes. They approved of this butchery. This was her final gift to them. Maybe they really were letting her leave.

"We have to go now," she said again.

She pulled her lover close and together they hurried across the field into the forest neither of them had ever traveled before, away from the town, away from his home, away from her home.

"We made it," Choushichi said. He was bent over, hands on his knees, catching his breath, long hair curtaining his face.

Sasa noticed he had lost his walking stick. She'd have to find him another one. She glanced behind him at the wall of dark trees. They'd made it through to the other side, traveled all night long. The sky was starting to lighten on the horizon and the chirr of night insects was being replaced by birdsong.

"We did, didn't we?" Sasa said, not believing it herself.

Choushichi stood up and brushed back his sweaty hair. The predawn blue illuminated his marred skin, his half smile, that faraway stare. He was beautiful.

As if reading her mind, he suddenly laughed a short buoyant chuckle that reminded her of their first days together, how clandestine it had been, and yet so very simple.

She looked down, suddenly embarrassed by her appearance. He couldn't see, but...Sasa shrugged off the tattered yukata; the obi was long torn from her waist and the smooth blue hemp of the garment ruined and shredded from the fight and the hundreds of catching branches she'd endured. Her hair, too, had fallen.

She reached up to tuck a strand behind her ear. The sound of bells. The gold comb! She untangled it and pinned back the bothersome tress. The comb, she thought, as delicate as it was, it had survived everything. A good omen for sure.

Choushichi heard the sound, too. His hands reached in her direction.

Sasa's heart raced. She licked her lips until the crusted blood became soft again. She led her lover's trembling fingers first across her stomach—a reminder—and then brought them to the sides of her face. Sasa waited to be pulled in, to be kissed.

His mouth was everything she missed and everything she wanted. There was nothing else. A feathery excitement stirred inside her. This must be how a human feels, she thought.

A sudden crack sounded from the forest and the couple started. The purposeful snap of a heavy branch. Choushichi's walking stick? She closed her eyes and inhaled. But she already knew. When she opened them again they were there, dozens of them lurking in the tree line, breaths spoiling the early morning air.

Her oldest brother stood two strides closer to her than the others. His chest was heaving, his lips flattened against his long, glinting teeth. So he hadn't listened to their mother, and Sasa's gift hadn't been enough.

She stared over Choushichi's shoulder into her brother's tawny eyes. He didn't make a sound. None of them did. Was he going to try and bring her home?

Choushichi tensed. He must have felt them, too, or perhaps he sensed her fear?

"They're back?" he whispered. "There are more?" Sasa realized he thought the new intruders were townspeople; another throng come to drive them farther away. She nodded and Choushichi recognizing the movement, dropped his hands.

Sasa refused to break her gaze with her eldest brother. She'd never stared at him this long. It was disrespectful. But there was no way she was going back. Her brother's fury, though, was building. She could feel it. His flaring nostrils, his fists clenching at his sides. It weakened her, hollowed her from the inside out. This time she was the one who didn't stand a chance.

And then his glare shifted, before meeting her eyes again. Choushichi. All at once she understood what he meant to do. What they all meant to do. They blamed Choushichi for her leaving. They hadn't come to bring her back. Sasa's insides roiled when she remembered the vicious way her brothers slaughtered their enemies and the slow, vulgar joy they took in it.

"It'll be okay," Sasa whispered, the words choking as they came out, at the realization that there had never been an escape.

"I'll take care of it." She was still staring at her brother when she said the words. His look of contempt turned into a smile. He understood.

"Okay," Choushichi said. He trusted her. He had always trusted her. She had never let him down before. "Be careful."

Sasa reached up and plucked the gold ornament from her hair. It's ethereal music ringing out again. Only yesterday night it had sounded like a promise. Hope.

"Here." She placed the belled comb in Choushichi's palm and he closed his hand around it. The song stopped as his fingers silenced the tiny chimes. A slow closing fist sealed also around Sasa's throat. She kissed him once more on the mouth.

Choushichi's brows knitted as a look of confusion passed over his face. His blind eyes glistened. It always looked like he was about to cry, she thought.

"I'll take care of it," she repeated.

Her brothers began to advance, each soundless stride closing the distance. They would be on her in seconds.

Sasa's fingers slipped around the back of her lover's neck, cupping it gently. His hair was still warm and damp with sweat. How many times had she kissed that scarred flesh? Her thumb settled under his chin. She closed her eyes.

Choushichi didn't struggle. Maybe he knew what was going to happen and accepted it, or maybe he didn't even suspect what she had to do. It didn't matter really.

Eyes squeezed shut; Sasa felt the growing heat of her brothers as they neared, her skin prickling with the immense weight of them. A thick, muscled arm swinging out, greedy jaws snapping. They were that close now.

Sasa took a deep breath, and in the expanding silence that numbed her mind she said goodbye. With one quick motion she snapped her wrist and Choushichi crumpled. Sasa fell to one knee with him, guiding his body carefully to the ground.

When she opened her eyes again she concentrated only on straightening her lover's robes, sweeping away dirt from the coarsely woven material, and touching his lips over and over until she was sure that not another breath would be drawn in or whispered out.

He was gone.

The only sound now was the roaring of blood in her ears. The thundering of it hushed everything. There was no birdsong, no wind in the trees, no crackle of leaves under anxious foot.

With no comb to pin her hair, it hung again wild about her face. She imagined she looked like some animal or monster even. Sasa slowly got to her feet and turned to face her brothers. Her muscles trembled, readying as she stood to her full height, filled her lungs, and squared her shoulders.

She used both hands to brush her fallen hair up and behind the horns that were now long enough to keep the tresses back. She met her oldest brother's poisonous stare. Something wretched boiled inside her, both sick and excited about this moment and about the moments that were soon going to come rushing in at her. The unknowable future. This is a feeling that no human has ever felt, Sasa thought. She laughed from a belly alive, and lunged.

FOUR GUYS WALK INTO A BAR

"*Isoide*! Hurry!" Hana, the seventy-three-year-old owner-cook-waitress of Sumikko, presses the phone to her ear with one hand, while with her other she scoots a heavy fry pan across the metal grate and flicks her wrist. A wokful of fried rice takes flight and then cascades back into the sizzling pan. "This needs to be taken care of immediately."

Hana tucks the phone into the folds of the tightly wrapped obi around her waist. As she tips the fried rice onto a ceramic dish, a whoof of garlic-scented steam envelops her face and neatly pinned chignon.

"*Hai, douzo*," she says, tottering over to the table where three

51

gaijin sit in deep and noisy conversation.

"Thank you, *doumo*," says the redhead with the sesame seed-tossed freckles all over his face and neck, arms and hands. He takes the dish without looking at her and sets it down roughly in front of his friends. He starts talking again.

"Shit, man, I can't take it anymore." The redhead, his name is Mikey, scrubs his hands back and forth through his curls. He reaches for his half-empty beer and swigs. "I think I'm going to snap."

"No, you're fine. You're cool. What's the problem?" Spencer sits across from him. He's the one with the dark hair and shaggy neck beard. He winks at Jolly, the third friend, the one who has considerably less fucks to give about everything. Jolly raises his eyebrows, but doesn't wink back.

Although Mikey and Spencer are the same age—twenty-two—Neck-Beard Spencer looks at least ten years older. There's the weary sag around his eyes, there's the unfortunate early-onset pattern baldness, there's the daily growing paunch.

"It's just everything, I guess." Mikey waves a hand to indicate the bar, a tiny *izakaya* nestled in some backstreet alley of Roppongi. Mikey's not even sure where—he gets lost every time he tries to find it. Thank God for the GPS on his phone.

"The furniture's too short." Mikey slaps the low *kotatsu* table they're sitting around. He examines the illegible brush and ink scribbles on long rectangles of yellowing paper that line the walls. Low ceiling. Blackened wood beams. A giant porcelain cat, one paw raised, has been staring at him all night long. "Nothing makes any freaking sense."

He takes another drink from his mug of beer. It helps him contemplate.

"Is this what they call culture shock?" Mikey asks. "Like what the hell? Who puts corn on pizza? Corn on pizza, Christ."

"I pick it off." Jolly is sitting cross-legged with his back against a Showa Era-looking beer poster, a pastel-colored woman in a kimono holding up a bottle of Kirin. *Drink Kirin for a Brighter Day.* Jolly's the surfer-hippie of the three, shoulder-length sandy-blond hair, an all-year tan, and a scar through one eyebrow where a board clipped him once. To his left sulks freckled Mikey and across from Mikey, the animated Spencer.

"Is that all that's bothering you?" Spencer asks, stroking his beard. "Because I got some awesome news that's going to totally make you feel better."

"There's something wrong with me. I don't want to be mad all the time, but I am," Mikey says. "Or depressed, or something. Is this what depression feels like?"

Hana shuffles back over on slippered feet and sets down a green glazed platter. On the platter rest eight perfectly round balls, all slathered in sweetened brown sauce with a thin zigzag of mayonnaise, a handful of writhing dried fish shavings, and a pinch of powdered *nori* on top of that.

"*Hai, takoyaki,*" the old woman says and places a stack of small saucers on the corner of the table for them to use. Neck-Beard Spencer indicates another round of beers and she hurries back to the bar.

"And this." Mikey points to the newly delivered dish. "Who calls their food *yucky*? Takoyucky. It doesn't make sense."

Jolly reaches over, tweezers one of the crispy-on-the-outside, mushy-on-the-inside balls with his chopsticks, and pops it in his mouth. He chews, open mouthed, sucking in air to cool the food.

"Seriously, what is this shit?" Mikey pushes the plate between Spencer and Jolly.

"Are you kidding me? This shit is the shit," Spencer says. He nudges one of the balls onto a saucer and slices it in half with his chopsticks.

"No, this shit *is* shit." Mikey crosses his arms.

"Listen, you'll get used to it," Spencer says. "I got used to it. I've got two years on you. I'm what they call a long-timer. This is just a phase. I mean you've only been in Japan three months. This is normal. Right, Jolly?"

"Some people don't assimilate," Jolly answers. He's paying attention to refilling his tiny *ochoko* cup from a large, almost-full *ishobin* saké bottle. Jolly doesn't drink beer.

Spencer chooses to ignore the remark.

"Mikey, I promise you, you're going to lose ten pounds and get healthy. You'll go back to Omaha and be like, *Steak*? Where's the sushi? Look at me, I don't hardly even eat meat anymore."

"Man, you've gained at least twenty pounds since we graduated. Hell, that was only two years ago." Mikey cocks his head and raises an eyebrow, looking his friend up and down.

"Well, you know, I've been hitting the gym." Spencer pulls at the front of his shirt, massages a bicep. He glances down at the belly bulge and tries to suck it in. He thinks about buying some new clothes. Do they sell clothes his size on Amazon.jp?

Jolly's smile is only seen by Hana who has arrived at the table with two new mugs of beer. She sets them down and carries the empties away.

"Anyway, forget all that for a minute. I've got a surprise. This is huge. Are you ready?" Spencer waits for a reluctant yes from his friend. "Okay, the thing is, I know a guy who knows a guy who teaches ninjutsu. I'm talking the real deal. Not this namby-pamby stuff you see back home."

"Oh yeah?" Mikey sounds only mildly interested in the huge surprise. He runs a finger over the foam on his beer in an attempt to deflate the bubbles quicker.

"But it's really secretive and all. I think I'm going to be able to get us an introduction next month," Spencer says. "In Japan you can't just go knocking on a master's door, right? You know what I'm talking about. So, dude, bro, you can't bail now."

"I don't know," Mikey says. "I have zero spare cash. I'm just thinking of saving up for a few more months and ditching this place. Screw my contract. Screw corn on pizza and octopus balls and me having to change my slippers when I go to the bathroom."

"Mikey, no. The dream, remember the dream." Spencer holds up a fist across the table. "Mikey, Michelangelo. Remember seventh grade? We made a pact. Cowabunga."

"Cowabunga," Jolly repeats and finishes off the contents of his tiny cup in one swig. He pours another.

Two businessmen walk into the bar, greet Hana, and sit at the farthest table from the three expats.

"Yeah, I haven't forgotten," Mikey says. "But maybe things are different. I'm different."

"Ninjutsu, dude. Back-fist-spinning-corkscrew punch." Spencer throws out a particularly well-executed karate chop-block-punch move he's been perfecting for the past five years. He's convinced it's one of the most perfect techniques ever dreamed up. He thinks it's deadly. "I've found our Splinter, man. I've found him."

"French fries," Mikey says, turning the menu over and over. "Is it too much to ask for french fries?"

"McDonald's," Jolly says. "Every corner."

Just then the door to the izakaya slides open so fast it bounces back and hits the new customer on the shoulder. The new customer, all six feet three of him, ducks through the *noren* curtain and clips his cowboy hat so that it almost falls off. He rights it with his free hand, spots his three friends, and galumphs over.

"Yo! You won't believe what just happened to me," the new guy, Deke, says as he plops down on the raised sitting area and awkwardly removes his boots.

"Let's see, you knocked your hat off for the one-hundredth time?" Spencer guesses.

"Yeah, no," Deke says, a moment of confusion crosses his face before he finds his original thought again. "This! This happened to me." He holds up a Hello Kitty bento-*bako* by the plastic handle.

"Lunch happened to you?" Jolly asks.

"No, shh. Be discreet." Deke scoots in at the table, nudging Spencer over so that now Spencer's sitting in front of Jolly and Deke's in front of Mikey. The cowboy gaijin sinks his long legs into the cutout hole under the kotatsu.

"Discreet? You're carrying a pink Hello Kitty bento box, man," Spencer says.

"*Jouki, hitotsu, kudasai*!" Deke yells to Hana, absolutely mangling the pronunciation as he does.

Hana is standing behind the bar turning long onion and chicken skewers over a mini charcoal grill. Every so often she removes them one by one and dips them into a container of savory sauce before slapping them, steaming and popping, back onto the flames to cook some more.

She has never really understood why foreigners flock to Sumikko. It started about five years ago when a couple of guys discovered the beer was cheap, the food was cheap, and the kotatsu tables all had big spaces where they could dangle their long gaijin legs. A pleasant Japanese atmosphere with none of the prickly limbs that came from sitting on the floor. She wonders how much it would cost to have the holes covered over.

Hana brings over a beer, a small bowl of edamame, and a hot hand towel so the new customer can wipe his hands.

"*Arigatou*," is Deke's twangy response.

Hana bows her retreat and nods at the two businessmen and the only other person in the bar besides the four foreigners, a woman in a suit sitting at the far corner typing on her laptop. She has looked up to see who is making the noise. She nods back at Hana. Deke sees the action and misinterprets it. He tips his hat in the woman's direction and smiles his most irresistible smile. He thinks his gold-capped incisor makes him look a little dangerous and sexy. He winks. The woman rolls her eyes and returns to her work.

"I think she's into me," Deke says to his friends.

"See," Spencer goes on, returning to the conversation with Mikey. "Take Deke here. If anyone was *not* going to fit in Japan, it'd be him. There's this huge cowboy who didn't even graduate high school. There's…there's…" Spencer cannot for the life of him think of something positive to say about his cowboy-style friend.

"The adorably churlish nature," Jolly adds. "The unmistakable reek of misogyny."

"Yeah, that," Spencer agrees. "Just look at him. His students adore him. They keep telling him how Japanese he is, how he's more Japanese than Japanese."

"Thank you, Spencer. Thank you, Jolly." Deke bows his head so low that he nearly loses his hat again. Another close call. He then places his Stetson pinch front lovingly on a flat pillow behind him, picks off a few pieces of lint. It's an expensive hat. The most expensive thing he's ever owned. He loves this hat.

Jolly raises his cup to the big man.

"So what's in the box?" Mikey asks.

"Oh yeah, this!" Deke waits for Hana to get all the way back behind the bar and into the kitchen before he speaks.

"So, yeah, so I was just finishing up a private class and I'm walking down the alley here, just about to open the door, when this guy jumps right out of the shadows, like out of nowhere, and he's like all *suimasen*, can you help me, and I'm like all *nan desu ka?*"

"Was he trying to sell you a phone card?" Mikey asks.

"No, no. He was selling…" Deke surveys the room, looks over his shoulder. The three strangers in the bar—the businessmen and the lady at the computer—couldn't be less interested in the man in the cowboy hat and his Hello Kitty lunchbox.

Deke pushes the bento to the middle of the table, scooting aside, as he does, half-eaten plates of crispy fried *kara-age* chicken and silky smooth, cold tofu topped with shredded ginger and chopped spring onion. He makes eye contact with each of his friends, one at a time. This is his way of indicating the importance of the situation. This is how he lets them know they are to take him seriously now. He takes a deep breath.

"It's an alien," Deke says.

Mikey, Spencer, and Jolly erupt in laughter.

"Are you high?" Spencer asks, trying to catch his breath.

"No, man, there was something about this guy in the alley. Something in his look," Deke says. "He was dressed really odd, like from some old-fashioned samurai flick, but some of the threads in his kimono were glowing, this silver buzzing color. Buzzing!"

"Silver buzzing color?" Mikey asks.

"You are high," Spencer says.

Jolly wipes away a tear with his knuckle.

"No, shut up, man. It wasn't just him. I saw it. He showed it to me."

The three quieted and almost began to take their cowboy friend seriously.

"So, what you're telling us is that you bought ET and have him right there in your Hello Kitty bento box?" Spencer asks.

"That's what I've been saying." Deke rubs the top of the shiny plastic lid.

"How much?" Mikey asks.

"Five hundred yen," Deke admits. "And can you keep your voice down? The guy made me promise not to tell anyone."

"That's, what, five dollars?" Mikey asks.

"Yeah, man," Spencer replies. "Five bucks for a real live alien."

More laughter.

"Don't worry, no one here speaks English except us," Spencer reassures. "Let's see it."

Deke unclips and slides off the plastic carrying band. The glossy Hello Kitty face is staring up at them, throwing a peace sign and winking an eye. *Happy Lunch Ready Smile*, reads the script.

Deke takes a long swig of beer. He rests his giant palm on the lid. "Ready?"

"Just get it over with," Spencer says.

With one hand Deke lifts off the lid and sets it aside.

There is a brief moment of utter silence as all four men lean forward and crane their necks to better see into the black depths of the box.

Explosive laughter.

"What the fuck, man," Spencer says, banging the table. "You got taken. Five hundred yen?"

Jolly chuckles and reaches for his drink.

"Wait, what?" Deke is the only one still examining the insides of the box where the alien rests. What he's looking at is a sushi-sized dollop of orange mush.

"It's a piece of *uni* man. Sea urchin," Spencer says. "Someone sold you their lunch. Jolly was right." He holds his beer up to recognize the quiet man against the wall.

"That's what I've been saying," Mikey adds, seeing an opportunity to start in on all that is wrong with Japan again. "Who eats sea urchin eggs? That's not right."

"Actually they're gonads," Jolly says. "They produce the milt that—"

"That's even *more* not right!" Mikey yells and pulls at his curly red hair again.

"So someone scraped some uni off a piece of sushi and told you it was an alien." Spencer makes air quotes around the word *alien*. "And you bought it for five hundred yen. Worse things have happened."

"No, man, no." Deke shakes the box. "It was moving when he showed it to me. It has these little eyes and a little face and this little…"

"You really are high," Mikey says. He reaches for a new pair of chopsticks from the bamboo cup and snaps them in two. "I'll give you your five hundred yen back if you eat it."

"Don't joke about that. You don't know how old it is. You could get parasites," Spencer says. "My aunt in Albuquerque once ate some bad *hamachi* and got parasites." Spencer made the sign of the cross.

"Oh, man, I didn't know," Mikey says.

"We don't like to talk about it."

Mikey allows a moment of silence to commemorate the aunt in Albuquerque, then starts back in on Deke.

"I'm no expert on sushi, but this one looks pretty fresh if you ask me," Mikey encourages. "Slap some wasabi on that puppy and chow. I'll give you a thousand yen. You'll make money."

"Fuck you if you think I'm eating that thing," Deke says. He pouts. Nurses his beer.

Mikey uses the chopsticks and flips the carrot-colored, pebbly mass over.

"What the hell is that?" Spencer's voice goes up an octave. He's pointing with one hand and covering his mouth with the other.

All four lean back over to gaze into the box.

"It's an eye," Deke says. "I told you. I told you."

"That's not an eye," Jolly insists.

"Touch it," Spencer says.

"I'm not touching it." Deke withdraws his finger that was almost touching it. "Maybe it's a mouth."

"That's not a mouth." Jolly pulls away and reclaims his place against the wall.

"Maybe it's a butt," Mikey says in a voice that would do the most immature schoolboy proud.

"Wait, do sea urchins' man-parts have mouths?" Deke asks.

"Hell if I know," Spencer says.

"You're all big boys with iPhones. Wikipedia," Jolly adds and starts to thumb his own phone. He's not looking up the biology of sea urchins, however. He's looking up train times.

"Here, let's try this." Mikey holds his chopsticks one in each hand like a surgeon and begins a layman's dissection.

"Stop! You're hurting it," Deke says.

"Don't be an idiot." Spencer chuckles.

"The fuck?" Mikey jumps, regains his composure, and starts prodding again. "There's a bone in there. Or cartilage or something."

"Jolly, Google sea urchin and cartilage," Spencer insists.

Jolly ignores him and sets the alarm on his phone for the latest possible time he can leave the izakaya to make his train back to Shinjuku. It's never a good idea to get stuck in Roppongi all night long.

"You're making a mess. Here." Spencer pours some of his beer onto the dissected spongy chunk. He adds some soy sauce for good measure.

"Look what you did." Deke yanks the bento box toward him and guards it with both hands. "Cut it out."

Spencer and Mikey laugh.

"Alien soup." Spencer makes a slurping noise.

"You guys suck," Deke says. With one arm protectively

wrapped around the bento-bako he finishes his mug of beer in two long draws and shouts for another.

There's an awkward silence as the friends try to find that place where they all get along again. Hana brings over the new beer, takes the empty. After she leaves, Spencer tries normal conversation again.

"So my idea was that we could train here for a couple years under Master Suzuki-sensei."

"Master Suzuki-sensei?" Jolly interrupts, raises one eyebrow.

"Yeah, that's his name," Spencer says. "Anyway, we could train with him for a couple years, then go back to the States and open our own ninjutsu school."

"Yeah, maybe, I guess," Mikey says.

"We'll call it Now-You-See-Me, Now-You-Don't Ninja Academy," Spencer says.

Jolly chokes on his drink and wipes his mouth with the back of his hand. He picks up the large saké bottle and pours another, this time into his water glass. He stoppers it and pushes it away. He doesn't need to be drinking this much. He knows this. He wishes he could stop this.

"The fuck, man!" Deke jumps and bangs both of his giant knees against the low table.

On the other side of the room, the woman in the suit closes her computer, pays her bill, and leaves. She's seen too many drunken foreigners. She doesn't need to see any more.

"What the hell?" Deke reaches for the wet towel and begins wiping a place on the back of his hand.

"What?" Spencer looks genuinely confused.

"You know what you did."

The two businessmen are out the door as well. Hana's izakaya, Sumikko, used to be a nice place. Cheap beer, cheap food, quiet. All her *jouren*, the regular customers, sitting around chatting about their quiet lives. Now she stands behind the bar, filling another mug of beer and wondering if the four men are going to order any more food or should she start cleaning the grills.

"I don't. What?" Spencer glances from Jolly to Mikey and back again.

"You put that alien thing on the back of my hand when I wasn't looking." Deke is now scouring his forearm, the skin an angry red.

"Are you insane? I've been sitting here talking to you the whole time."

Jolly tips up the bento box to show the others. It's empty.

"Hey, where'd it go?" Mikey asks.

"You tell me, asshole," Deke says, glaring and scrubbing, scrubbing, scrubbing. "It was one of you, one of you did it."

"Maybe you accidentally ate it," Spencer jokes, but Deke is still working fiercely on his skin. No one laughs.

There is a second when Spencer rolls his eyes at Mikey and circles his ear with one finger. Mikey laughs uncomfortably, but he's not really concerned with Deke right now. He's weighing his options in life: opening a ninjutsu school against going back to community college to learn a real skill. He always thought he'd be good in graphic design. Jolly, on the other hand, sips at his drink.

He's glassy-eyed; his head has taken on a pleasant spin. He's thinking of a boy back home he might still be in love with.

"Fuck you." Deke is suddenly motionless. His big head tilted down, he's glaring out the tops of his eyes. His voice is barely audible.

"What?" Spencer looks up.

"I said, fuck you, man."

"Hey, dude—" Spencer is smiling a forced smile. Both Mikey and Jolly are now fully present and realize something very bad is about to happen.

Deke leaps to his feet, one knee clipping the table and sending dishes and drinks sliding. He reaches down and grabs the tinted saké bottle by the neck and points the heavy end at his friend sitting right beside him.

"Hey, man." Spencer starts doing a kind of frantic jazz hands. "It's cool. It's cool."

Deke is having none of that. He slowly pushes the bottle into Spencer's chest, making the chubby, bearded man scuttle backward until he is pinned against the wall.

"Why the fuck you always riding me? What the fuck is always so funny?" Deke is hunched over, screaming the words through a mouth full of froth. His eyes don't look right.

"Ha," Deke says. He doesn't really laugh. He just says the word and stands to his full height, takes the neck of the bottle in both hands, and brings it back, high over his shoulder like a baseball bat.

All three sitting men have the same two thoughts in

succession: first, that Deke is a giant at six foot three, the biggest they've ever seen him; and second, that the amount of force delivered on impact if this giant, their friend, should choose to swing that bottle would be devastating.

"Hey, come on, dude, chill." Spencer eases up on one knee until he's almost standing. Deke takes in the movement, loads his stance, and mutters something indecipherable.

"I didn't mea—," were Spencer's last words.

Deke's tensed body releases, his hips turn, and the bottle swings. It catches Spencer right above the ear with an awful sound. The man with the unkempt neck beard and the too-early beer belly crashes onto the table.

Both Jolly and Mikey try to register the absolute absence of movement, a life completely vanished in an instant. One of them thinks the saddest thing of all is that Spencer never even had the chance to execute his back-fist-spinning-corkscrew punch.

Mikey pisses himself while Jolly ignores the body crumpled on the table in front of him and instead marvels at the beautiful spray of blood fanned out across the wall. It starts where Spencer was sitting seconds before and stretches four tables down and even up into the wooden rafters of the old izakaya. The woman in the faded beer poster has a red tear running from the corner of one eye to her ear. Jolly looks down and sees even his own body is perfectly speckled.

Mikey lets out a mewling sound that brings both Jolly's and Deke's attention to him.

Deke turns to face Mikey across the table, the gore-covered

bottle now pointing at his freckled friend. Chest heaving, face engorged a dangerous ruddy red. The large man is gurgling, something wet is making its way up his throat. The veins on his neck and forehead stand out in the most delicate blue. A summer sky on a coconut-scented beach, Jolly thinks.

The dreaminess suddenly fades from Jolly's eyes and he jumps to his feet and tries to pull the younger man, the smallest one, the newbie with the mass of unruly red curls, up. He's attempting to move him away from what he knows is going to happen. The whole time Jolly is trying to find the right words to defuse the situation. But there are no right words. He knows this, too. He knows exactly what is going to happen.

The bottle comes down again. This time from above. Jolly drops onto Mikey's urine soaked lap, pinning him to the *tatami* mat floor.

Mikey's mouth is open, bottom lip trembling hard. He's not going anywhere. He remembers his mom, remembers the sound of her old floppy slippers padding down the hall, around the kitchen. He smells pancakes and syrup. He hates Japanese food. He wants some sweet buttery pancakes with so much syrup they swim in it. There is a flash of movement and then everything turns off.

Deke is alone now. His gurgling grows worse. He drops the bottle, claws at his throat, pinches at his tongue with fingers that are numb and no longer belong to him. He collapses, a knee crushing his favorite cowboy hat. The one he is so proud of. If he was in his right mind he might mourn the loss of the hat, he might wonder where all this sticky fluid in his mouth and nose was coming from, he might try to spit it out. Cough. But Deke was dead three minutes ago. Now his body thrashes and kicks and stills.

The door to the izakaya slides open, quietly this time. An old man with mussed up hair and dressed in a worn *hakama* and hemp shirt enters; the threads in the cloth buzz silver. He nods to Hana and proceeds to the table where the four men lie tangled and motionless. He steps his way through the mess, careful not to dirty his tightly woven sandals while removing another small bento box from the deep pocket at his side. With a thumb, he pops off the lid and presses the empty container against Deke's hand.

The spongy, orange mass releases itself from the bone and the meat and all the fluids in the man's body, and rises to the surface of the skin again. Two eyes like black seeds twinkle and observe the stranger. A quick shiver, and it hops into the box.

"Good boy," the man coos. "*Ii-ko*, good boy."

The orange creature churrs and mewls as the man replaces the lid and slips it back into his pocket.

Carefully he steps back through the carnage to where Hana is wiping down the counter. She's already turned off the grill and has decided to take the yakitori skewers home for a late-late dinner. She imagines she'll be hungry by the time she gets home.

"I'll send over the others to clean this right up," the man says.

Hana bows and smiles. She doesn't have to say a word. She

follows the plodding man to the door, watches his softly glowing back as he makes his way down the narrow alley.

Hana reaches up on her tiptoes and lifts off the rod holding the noren curtain. The faded cloth reads *Sumikko.* The izakaya is now closed. She steps back inside, tired. It's been another one of those too-long nights. She makes her way back to the bar, thinking about bringing one of the more expensive bottles of saké home with her as well as the yakitori. She turns off the grill and readies to leave. From across the room Jolly's cell phone alarm starts to beep.

GO-AWAY MONKEY

"A monkey! A monkey!" a handful of broken children cried as they stumbled along the raised embankment, heading toward the town's center.

A monkey?

Okappa, trapped beneath the weight of the vile man Fuhaku, puzzled at why they were so excited. The animals weren't uncommon. They snuck into town all the time in search of food or to misbehave. What was so special about this particular monkey?

Fuhaku groaned and another group of townspeople, wheezing and dragging withered limbs, scuttled by. Not one of them—not the children or the adults—noticed Okappa and the noisy man struggling in the freshly cut, still-wet rice field below.

Why didn't he finish already? Okappa squirmed and bucked under the man's sweaty weight. But he only chuckled, got a better grip on her long hair, and pinned her once more to the muddy ground.

She couldn't leave yet. Timing. Sometimes she thought it was her luck that kept her alive this long. Other times, her timing.

While she waited, Okappa saved her strength and considered the depth of the glaze-blue autumn sky above. The way the townspeople suddenly shuffled around today—more animated, more aware—spurred a nervous scratching under her ribs. And now a monkey, she thought. A monkey.

Just then, in the sky beyond the man's ramming shoulder, a flock of cranes flew, parting clouds that immediately knitted back together in the birds' wake. *Ichi, ni, san.* The girl counted three more than last year. Fledglings. A resolve tightened in her gut, something to look forward to. Tomorrow she'd head out early and spend all day in the marshlands watching the animals feed and play.

"Such a pretty, pretty girl." Fuhaku nuzzled her neck and let go of her hair. His stench, raw and boar-like, clung to the back of her throat. She guessed it would stay there all day long. Gradually his weight increased as it always did after he exhausted himself.

Without the pig-like grunting in her ear, she could hear it now, in the distance, a jangle of bells echoing off the surrounding foothills. That's when she understood what the clamor was about.

"Such a pretty..." Fuhaku's breath was hot and smelled of

vinegar. His voice was growing sleepy. "Such a pretty, pretty girl."

Now it was time to go.

"Do you hear that?" Okappa kicked herself out from under the large man. Squelching through the mud, she got far enough away so that he couldn't grab her and yank her back. That had happened far too many times. She'd learned her lesson.

The faraway bells were getting closer.

"A stranger is here," she said. "It sounds like it might be a *saru-mawashi*, a monkey show."

Fuhaku sat up, legs splayed. His brow furrowed as he considered her words. A second later his slack face brightened and he leapt to his feet.

"A monkey!" He thrust two fingers into the obi that had loosened after slipping from his meaty belly up to his coward's chest. He withdrew a small gray river stone.

"*Kore kureru,*" he said. "I give this to you." He tossed the rock at her feet and then, after giving her a playful kick in the side, scrambled up the bank to join the quickly growing procession.

Monster, Okappa thought, standing. Pox-infested, pithy-brained, wretched monster. She slapped at her work kimono, attempting to knock off as much of the clinging mud as she could. One day she'd own a beautiful garment, something that didn't scratch her skin, something as soft as the tufts of crane down she collected from the fields after the birds frolicked. She believed the tufts held magic and gathered the fuzzy down, keeping it hidden at all times in the long dangling sleeves of her robe.

Okappa plucked the smooth stone from the ground and placed it on her tongue. She rolled it around in her mouth, the hardness softening as it clicked against her teeth. She held it in the hollow of her cheek and counted. *Ichi, ni, san.* She wished again that her magic wasn't so tiny, practically useless.

After checking to make sure she hadn't lost her sickle, she slipped her hand into the hemp pouch on her hip and withdrew a handful of fragrant, freshly harvested Shepherd's Purse. She spat the stone, now a soft and sticky candy, into her palm and covered it with the frilly leaves. She then tucked the treat into the unstitched opening on her collar and carefully worked it down.

It was a shame how many sweetmeats she'd lost to street urchins and thieves and otherwise friendly neighbors. Sometimes she swore everyone here could smell food, no matter how well hidden.

Okappa climbed from the field and folded into line behind the *geta* maker's wife. There, on the woman's back, secured by a long *onbuhimo* made of dirty gauze, were her twin daughters. Okappa tried not to notice how their dark, lifeless heads bounced in perfect time to the woman's steps, or how the woman still sang them lullabies and shushed them, despite the fact they hadn't made a sound in over a week.

As the throng neared the center of town they fanned out, gathering close, but not crossing the line the stranger was etching into the ground with his belled walking stick. He was drawing a giant circle.

His stage, Okappa thought.

74

In the middle of the ring stood the crumbling stones of the town's only well. Around the ring's outside edge there grew the stranger's audience, trembling and wheezing, hundreds of reedy legs, balancing bellies bursting with disease. It was terrible, but in the mass of dying flesh and heartbeats, Okappa noticed their eyes. In every single one, mucous filled or vacant, shone something she hadn't seen since the unfortunate wind blew in and ruined them all. It almost looked like hope.

The stranger finished his work and stood hands on hips to survey the crowd. Okappa marveled at the man. Under indigo robes of soiled but finely woven linen moved a body not crooked, not exhausted from his travels, not starving. In the rise of his shoulders and the turn of his waist there lurked power and certainty. It made Okappa nervous. She realized in her own body she could no longer distinguish hope from fear.

Before she could fall under his spell, though, her attention flitted. There, next to the well, was a pile of the man's bags and on top of that crouched the monkey.

He wore the same robe and bowl-shaped pilgrim's hat as his master; even donned matching woven sandals that laced up his twig-like legs. So tiny, Okappa thought, smaller than any of the creatures that descended from the mountains when hungry or mad. Was he a baby? But the face was different, too.

The stranger, seemingly satisfied with the number of people gathered, gave a hard yank on the long braided rope that ran from his belt to the monkey's ankle. Okappa cringed at the enervated squeak the animal made in reply to the order. She understood that reaction. She knew it well.

The monkey jumped and scurried to the stranger's side. He climbed up his robes and took a seat on his shoulder.

"Come merchant, farmer, father, and son!" The stranger paced the circle. He thumped the bottom of his staff on the ground, jingling the cluster of metal rings on top. "Come mother, daughter, come everyone."

Just then, across the crowd, Okappa spotted her grandfather, his gaze skipping from person to person, but oblivious to the spectacle by the well. He looked lost and afraid, and if she knew him as well as she thought she did, he looked like he was about to panic.

Okappa made her way over.

"*Ojiichan?*" she said, touching his shoulder, uncertain if it was him today or not. Her grandfather turned. His unfocused eyes cleared when he saw her.

"Look at you!" The old man threw both arms into the air and brought them down again so he could rub his hands together in that way that always made Okappa think of an elderly, sideways-leaning praying mantis.

"Shouldn't you be resting?" she asked. "How do you feel?"

"Oh, I'm just fine, as fine as yesterday and the day after that," he said and smiled his almost toothless grin.

"Are you hungry?" Okappa pressed her hand over the candy hidden in her robe.

She was relieved that her grandfather wasn't completely cloudy today, and she wanted to reward him when his memory was intact, at least in the moment. He took in her action, cut his eyes at the jostling, greedy crowd, and shook his head

"No, not at all. I just ate a big meal of salmon and pheasant and black beans." He slapped an imaginary belly and pretended to burp into his fist. Okappa felt terrible that he had to lie.

"But look at you." The old man pulled away to examine once more her clothes. "Did you fall again?"

Okappa laughed and looked down at her filthy work kimono. "Slipped on one of those jumbo *taneshi* snails."

"The pink ones?"

She nodded.

"Those are the nastiest."

"They are, aren't they?" She took his elbow and together they weaved their way through the suffering mass, apologizing as they went.

The sitting and crouching townspeople scowled and scooted aside. Old lady Tora spat at Okappa's feet while her husband slid a calloused hand up her kimono and squeezed her calf. Okappa pulled away and steered her grandfather to a place right behind the inscribed line where they took a seat.

"I don't understand. What's happening here?" her ojiichan asked, suddenly aware of his surroundings.

Okappa's smile felt weak on her lips. She remembered not five years ago when her grandfather had been a respected healer. He taught her everything she knew about wild grasses and roots. When the bad wind blew in, it was her ojiichan who left the town and traveled to faraway cities in order to bring back new medicines.

But none of them worked. The seeds of disease grabbed hold until even her grandfather—so wise and knowledgeable—lost his confidence. She watched helplessly as her last surviving family member crumbled. It wasn't the God of Pox that wrecked him. It was something almost more insidious that crept in and over time weakened his mind. Now she hardly recognized the man she'd looked up to for so many years.

"Watch," Okappa said and pointed to the stranger and his animal. She tried not to remember what happened to the last stranger who had wandered into their town.

"My name is Hanshiro of Edo and this tiny beast is Fukumimi," the stranger crooned.

With a flourish he grabbed the monkey from his shoulder and tossed him into the air. Fukumimi landed in the dirt. Two quick claps of Hanshiro's hands and the animal stood at attention, teeth bared, one furry shoulder peeking out from his skewed robe. Okappa wished she could pet him. She wondered if he would bite. She wondered if he was afraid. Hungry maybe?

Hanshiro mimicked the pose, standing straight, hands flat by his sides, a gruff clearing of his throat, and the two bowed in unison.

The townspeople clapped and whistled, wheezed and coughed. The anticipation of the show had enlivened them. It really had been a long time since they'd seen an outsider. Over a year. Two? No traveler dared come near their little corner of the world.

"Fukumimi and I have journeyed from the great city of Edo to the holy Mount Hiei where the Enraku Temple resides." Hanshiro made a sweeping motion toward the distant places he was talking about.

Okappa thought about the cranes earlier and remembered her talks with her grandfather when his mind was whole. She recalled the maps of far-off places he'd drawn for her with words. He used the hills and mountains she knew as guideposts. To the west lay Kyoto; in the east, past the faraway, snowy top of Mount Fuji, was Edo. The strange traveler, Hanshiro, was wrong. Mount Hiei was in the opposite direction.

"During our stay at Enraku-ji, we were fortunate enough to encounter a mountain *tengu* who imparted on us the secrets of an auspicious ritual," he continued.

"We are now on our way back to the magnificent Edo, but we thought we would share our good fortune with the towns and villages along the way."

The people cheered again. Okappa became aware that the growing hysteria smelled of burning honey and rotting fish. She brought her hands to her nose, fingers still fragrant from this morning's collected herbs, and took a deep breath. Tomorrow she'd go to the marshlands and watch the cranes play. It was a soothing thought.

Something hard bumped into Okappa's shoulder and she turned to see the town's carp-faced boy. The dreadful stunted thing was pointing at the monkey and bouncing on the balls of his feet, bug-eyes blinking, mouth popping open and closed, open and closed. She had never seen him so happy before. She smiled back and moved to pat him on the head. But before she could touch the child, two arms grabbed him away. His mother glowered at Okappa and hissed before disappearing with him into the crowd.

"What lovely children you have here," Hanshiro said. He took three long strides to the edge of his homemade stage and ruffled a small boy's thinning hair. The monkey gallop-hopped behind him, careful not to earn another tug on the leash. Okappa wondered why the man kept the rope looped and tucked so short at his waist. What was he afraid of?

"Are they very smart children?" Hanshiro asked.

It was an inquiry that sounded like an accusation. The people fidgeted and looked around.

"Of course they are." Hanshiro answered his own question and lightened the mood again. "Here's how I know." He held up a finger to indicate a grand idea. "I'll ask them a question and prove it to you."

He strode back to the well where he could be seen better by the surrounding audience. Two snaps of his fingers and Fukumimi scampered back onto the pile of belongings the stranger had lugged in on his back.

"What do we have here?" He motioned to the animal at his side. Fukumimi *ki-ki-ki*'d. His monkey shoulders stiffened and rose to his ears. He showed his teeth again, but this time the action resembled a smile.

"*Saru!*" the children cried.

"Saru," Hanshiro affirmed. He waved his hands and the monkey gracefully tumbled off the boxes and did a series of somersaults before returning to his perch. The children hooted and giggled. Okappa thought how sweet and clever the animal was and again had the urge to run up and pet him.

"A monkey, yes. A saru. And what other meaning does *saru* have?"

Before any of the children could answer, Okappa's grandfather shouted.

"Go away!"

Okappa was shocked at his rudeness, but the stranger didn't look offended. Instead he sauntered over to where she and her grandfather sat.

"Ah!" Hanshiro said. "The youngest heart in the group, I see."

Okappa's ojiichan beamed and began scratching nervously on his forearm. It was a habit she'd noticed he'd picked up several days ago. Tomorrow when she was out at the marshes she'd find some fishwort and make him a skin tincture.

Okappa ignored the banter between the two men and instead tried to get Fukumimi's attention. But the animal was shy and kept hidden behind his master's legs.

"Yes, then! *Saru* also means to go away!" Hanshiro boomed and strode back toward the center of his stage. That was when Okappa noticed the blood welling up on her grandfather's arm, the flesh scratched away like the thin delicate skin of a fish that had been grilled too long.

She gasped and seized his hand to stop him from causing any

81

more damage. She looked around for someone to help, but the others remained riveted on the stranger and his monkey. The few people who did witness the old man's injury and Okappa's distress all avoided eye contact. She'd have to do this, too, alone.

After finding the cleanest spot on her obi, Okappa used the sickle at her hip to cut off a bandage. She took a couple pinches from the precious downy crane feathers hidden in her dangling sleeve and pressed it into the wound. It was the only pure thing she owned and maybe it was magic. She then wrapped his arm and tied it.

"We need to get you home," Okappa said.

"No, no!" Her grandfather snatched his arm away. He had become mesmerized by the stranger and his pet.

"Go away!" Hanshiro shouted. "Everyone wants something to go away. Maybe it's the shriveled, insatiable claw of a poverty god, *binbogami,* lurking just over your doorstep, plucking away every good fortune before it enters your house." The man squatted and mimicked the miserable god everyone feared.

"Or perhaps it's something smaller, a festering tooth or an ancestor's spirit acting afoul." Hanshiro paused. "Maybe a bothersome mother-in-law."

There was an eruption of laughter and Okappa turned to watch the sea of black chortling holes, all expelling the last bit of air from their failing lungs as they remembered what sometimes happened to brutish mothers-in-law in their town.

"The seasons are changing." The tone of Hanshiro's voice was foreboding. "I hear it gets rather dire in towns like this. The snow can grow deep, and hunger torments with a renewed fury when it's winter."

Three times he struck the ground with his walking stick. *Ichi, ni, san.* The metal hoops on top jangled and the sky overhead grayed. A chilly wind kicked up and sent ice crackling through Okappa's bones. The near-constant coughing Okappa had grown used to soured to hacking and then retching.

"So this is my promise," Hanshiro began again. "If any of you good people could spare something, anything, a clink of coin, a whalebone *netsuke*, even a tarnished *kiseru* pipe that you no longer have use for, I will grant you one wish." Hanshiro raised that long finger once more.

"But here's the difference. Instead of giving you something, I will take something away. I will remove from you the thing you wish most to be rid of."

Was such a thing possible? Could he eliminate their suffering? This sickness? Okappa was about to change her opinion of the man when she glanced down and saw the heel of his sandaled foot firmly on the back of the monkey's head, keeping the animal's face pressed into the dirt, kowtowing, begging the town's good favor. Something vile and heavy bloomed in her chest. How could she have thought he was a good man?

"To accomplish such a feat, however, we must first transform this creature into the great god Sarutahiko. For those of you who wish to watch the transformation, please do, but don't forget to fetch your currency. We will begin the trade as soon as the dressing ceremony is completed." Hanshiro motioned to the sky with his staff. "It looks like the weather is growing foul. I think we should hurry. How about you?"

Hoarse whispers and slaps from wizened hands sent dozens of children flying from the mob to retrieve some perceived valuable that might be worthy enough to exchange for a wish.

Okappa watched the little ones scurry away. Were her neighbors really so desperate and blind that not a single one of them considered the imbalance of the stranger's deal?

"Now watch closely."

Hanshiro removed his foot from the animal's head. He clapped his hands twice and Fukumimi stood at attention, his arms extended from his sides, his chin up.

"Sarutahiko is one of the seven great gods," Hanshiro explained as he knelt and stripped the animal of its traveling clothes.

The monkey looked even smaller and more pitiful than before. His eyes darted from side to side, and Okappa was sure he was looking for a way to flee.

Timing, she wanted to tell it. If he was patient—infinitely patient—there would come the perfect time for him to escape. Timing or luck. Okappa felt weary carrying these thoughts for so long. But she had to. It was the only thing that kept her sane when everyone around her lost hope. Look what happened to them.

"Sarutahiko is also the symbol of strength and guidance. He clears the way, removes obstacles," Hanshiro continued.

"Let us say, he is a god that embraces many roles." The

stranger removed a boxwood comb from one of the lacquer boxes he'd retrieved from his bundles and ran it through Fukumimi's fur.

The monkey remained in the same upright position throughout the lengthy ceremony. Even as a greasy chunk of fragrant ambergris was massaged into his temples and chest; even as a tin was upturned and tapped with a fingernail until it sprinkled powder over his feet.

Okappa wondered how long he could endure the pose when next came a pair of tall, single-toothed geta. The shoes were explained, prayed over, and finally strapped firmly onto the animal's dusted feet. Fukumimi's legs trembled, but he didn't drop his arms or glance down.

Okappa wanted the whole show to stop already. She looked away, back at the ugly audience, rapt and waiting for the magic to happen. The children had begun returning from their errands and were slipping their pathetic treasures into their parents' hands. When the last child found his seat on the ground, there was a sudden gasp and a flurry of hands pointed toward the well.

Okappa turned in time to witness Hanshiro flourishing a garnet-colored silk kimono for all to see. Her breath swelled in her chest. She'd never seen anything so beautiful, not even in her most vivid dreams. It seemed to carry its own light in the fast-darkening sky.

Hanshiro threaded the animal's arms through the weighty sleeves, adjusting the cloth on his shoulders, smoothing it as he went. An amber-colored obi was then wrapped and twisted into an elaborate knot at the small of the animal's back. Hanshiro stood up and admired his work.

Fukumimi looked resplendent, balancing on the tall geta shoes, arms outstretched to fully display the intricate patterns of gold and black stitched into the shimmery red material. Okappa's chest ached at both the beauty and the sadness. Was she the only one who saw the animal's trembling tired limbs, and the length of rope still connecting its scarred foot to his master?

"As many of you might know, Sarutahiko is also an ancestor of the tengu, the mountain goblin." Hanshiro opened the last box. "It was because of my friend here we were given audience to the great tengu on Mount Hiei."

He produced a crimson mask and held it up for everyone to see. There was a simultaneous intake of breath. Thunder rumbled in the foothills and the air grew colder still. The storm the stranger had called was close. No one seemed to notice.

"You'll recognize the same long nose and ruddy face," Hanshiro pointed out.

Okappa wasn't sure if it was the detail of the mask that caused the gathering to balk or the ghoulish expression it held. A deeply furrowed brow creased its forehead while from its eyebrows and chin great shocks of stiff white hair flew like some unnatural beast. It looked alive, Okappa thought, more alive than even the people who surrounded her.

By far the worst feature of the mask, though, was its mouth. Even from the distance she could make out the yellow of two sharp fangs buried into a black-lipped grimace. It was an expression of absolute fury, horrifying. What kind of god was this?

"I give you the great Sarutahiko." Hanshiro placed the mask over the monkey's face and tied it securely.

He waited for the applause to cease before removing his *sandogasa*.

"Here we will accept your offerings." Hanshiro flipped the woven bamboo hat upside down so that it resembled a basket. He hugged it to his side with one arm.

"Shall we begin?" To Okappa's surprise, Hanshiro then pulled the coiled leash free from his belt, giving the fettered animal the freedom of the entire length of rope.

The man then snatched up his walking stick and began hitting it rhythmically on the ground again. With each jolt the cluster of rings on top sang out and more dark clouds rolled in.

He started a slow chant. The words were nothing Okappa had ever heard before, old Japanese or Chinese, or maybe some long-dead language known only to the gods. Discordant, wrong. Mesmerizing.

Fukumimi—now Sarutahiko—stood in the center of the ring near the well, stately, no longer fidgeting or swaying under the weight of the outfit. Had a real transformation taken place? Okappa imagined the tiny, frightened creature she had witnessed cowering behind his master's calves not ten minutes ago had vanished, and instead, there, donned in an awful mask and beautiful silks, breathed a god.

Excitement mingled with fear shivered goose bumps across

her skin. Could he really grant the town's wishes? And what would the town do if he couldn't?

Sarutahiko took his first step. Okappa held her breath, sure the creature would tumble off the precarious shoes and hurt himself. But he didn't. Instead every time he brought the single tooth of a geta down it seemed to bite into the earth, hold on.

Lift, move, hover, stab, he circled the perimeter of the stage. At least twenty paces behind, Hanshiro followed. The droning incantation and the constant ringing of metal on metal growing until the cacophony filled the darkening sky and turned the townspeople mad with hope and the promise of release from their hell. A flash of skeletal lightning lit up the hills in the distance. A growl of thunder.

Now it was the monkey who tethered the man, Okappa thought.

The little god bowed his masked head once, and stepped straight into the voracious mob. Immediately a tangle of arms—weeping flesh stretched flower-petal thin across splintering bones—shot out. But Sarutahiko remained erect, composed, and continued his stoic march. The only emotion betraying him was the mask as it sneered and ground its muscled jaws.

Weren't gods supposed to be compassionate?

Okappa waited anxiously as the two wove their way through the roiling mass. Her attention fell on Hanshiro dutifully hypnotizing the people and collecting their worthless trinkets in his upturned hat. She caught a hint of a smile on his face. A smirk. It almost looked like he was appraising each item as it tumbled in. So that's what this was really about.

Anger seethed in Okappa's chest. This man could not alleviate anyone's torment. He was a charlatan. It made her ache to witness what little effort it took to convince the utterly hopeless that their suffering wasn't in vain, that they were due their just reward. Happiness would be theirs again, but at a cost. These paltry tokens couldn't be enough. What else did the stranger want? Lift, move, hover, stab. Another step. The monkey turned again and Okappa could have sworn she saw the fiery eyes behind the mask flicker with recognition as they met hers. The expression changed and one corner of the frown pulled up into a half grin. She was overcome with the feeling that she knew this creature. Sarutahiko began his slow advance in her direction.

Without thinking, Okappa ran two fingers up the hem of her robe and found the lump of candy she'd hidden there earlier. As quickly as she could, she worked the treat through the rough material to the open seam, slipped it out, and cupped it in her palms.

She glanced around, seeing if the others could smell it and knowing what they'd do if they could. But it wasn't her neighbors that noticed her betrayal. It was her grandfather.

Ojiichan sat, cross-legged, not awed by the monkey god headed their way, but staring at her with lucid eyes.

For years this was their routine. Everyday she'd bring the treasures she earned home and present them to the elderly man over watery tea. Her grandfather would marvel at the shapes and colors of the sweets. A cherry blossom. A chrysanthemum. A peony. They changed depending on the season. She had no control over this.

At first he'd politely refuse the desserts, but she'd insist and then delight in watching him place the candy on his tongue and close his eyes as it melted away. He'd smile and exclaim it was the best thing he'd ever tasted, even better than yesterday's and the day after that. Okappa would laugh and relish in the joy of the moment. That alone was enough to sustain her.

Embarrassment burned her face and neck.

"I had a big lunch," her grandfather said, answering the unasked question.

He looked down and patted a belly that would never be sated again. This time when he smiled at her it was the most present she'd seen him in years.

"It's okay," he said. "I'm not hungry anymore."

He meant it, she thought.

All at once Okappa was knocked sidewise as the deranged crowd lunged back and forth. Sarutahiko was so close. Lift, move, hover, stab. His geta connected with the earth and the earth held him up. Another step closer. He stopped.

Okappa sat there on the ground, back straight, hands hiding the candy. In front of her the monkey god—his presence humming inside her head like a field of summer bees—upright in his single-toothed wooden shoes. The two were almost eye to eye.

Okappa inhaled and swooned. The scent of him brought back a childhood memory. Deep in the forest, trees shooting straight up where they knitted into latticework and sparkled down gems of sunlight that danced when the wind blew. She squatted in the crackling leaf fall with her grandfather, snapping the fleshy stalks of mushrooms and drinking in the dewy perfume of ferns and cedar and pine.

Okappa held out her cupped hands. Her gift wasn't for the stranger, Hanshiro, the man bent only on devouring her town and its people. Her gift was for him, the creature held captive.

The frenzy escalated. People crawled over one another, groaning with the effort, shrieking in pain. A heel found purchase in another's thigh. A head snapped back when a fist latched onto a handful of hair and pulled to gain height. On all sides, dozens of gnarled hands thrust toward the animal standing directly in front of Okappa.

It was then that she saw what was really happening. The townspeople weren't just stroking the creature and the extravagant garments for good luck, they were pinching away tufts of fur from the animal's exposed arms and legs. Its tender skin raw and swollen, bleeding.

They were consuming him. Did Hanshiro know this? Was this his plan all along? Was the animal a sacrifice? Bile rose in Okappa's throat. Her mind twisted. Who were these people? What had they become? She hated them all.

"This is for you." She pressed the leaf-covered sweetmeat into the animal's paws.

The monkey god held up the treasure and examined it. He picked away the thin leaves until the treat was revealed. A golden chrysanthemum. He looked back at her and the furious eyes behind the lacquered wood blinked and turned hazel again.

An arm shot out to snatch the food.

"Stop!" Ojiichan bellowed and the hand withdrew.

The grotesque throng swayed and seemed to consider its next move. Okappa looked around and felt the helpless panic of drowning when the realization hit her.

The townspeople were no longer separate individuals. They were connected. Limbs conjoined, skin fused. They had become a single raging beast full of fragile bird hearts all trapped inside heaving ribcages. Hungry and insane and greedy for its reward.

Why? Was it the horror of their shared memories that turned them? Or was it was the absolute futility of their useless lives?

The fingers continued to pick and pinch at Sarutahiko who remained still and enduring.

"Eat it," Okappa urged.

The monkey tried to push the fist holding the gold-tinted sugar candy under the tightly tied mask, but it wouldn't reach.

Okappa leaned forward and yanked at the cords and released the mask. There was no god underneath, only a small animal, his face damp with sweat, fear moving behind his eyes.

Okappa stood and threw the carved mask into the crowd opposite where Hanshiro, oblivious, was still chanting and assessing his plunder. The monster moaned and rippled in pleasure. She could feel its hunger increasing.

With the disguise removed, the monkey's movements were again quick and twitchy. He blinked up at her, the sugar candy clutched close to his silk-clothed chest. The little thing looked confused, like he had just woken from a dream into a nightmare.

Terrified. He wants to flee his fate. But we can't. None of us can.

Okappa bent over and slipped his tiny feet from the towering shoes and hurled them, too, into the beast. It bucked and undulated.

Immediately the monkey dropped to all fours and scampered across the line scratched into the earth, the line that delineated the profane world along the edges, from the holy one in the center.

Alone, halfway between the well and the thrashing beast, he sat on the ground, rich robes pooling about his body, and stuffed the treat into his mouth. He chewed and stared at Okappa with an emotion she couldn't read.

Starving. How long had it been since he'd eaten? Lightning crackled through the low black clouds and thunder boomed. The storm was almost on them. The monkey startled at the sound and bolted. He got as far as where the lacquer boxes lay, almost to the well, when he was stopped by the rope around his foot.

Feeling the pull, Hanshiro looked up.

"You!" he said. "What are you doing?"

He was pointing at Okappa, who was still standing among the mass of writhing bodies. His gaze took in the monkey— unmasked and small again—and then returned to the girl.

"How dare you?" he roared.

Hanshiro threw down the hat that fell heavily but spilled

nothing. With both hands he took up the leash tied to his waist and yanked hard. The monkey's leg was jerked out from under him and he went sprawling through the dirt, screeching.

Okappa cried out and the beast laughed from its countless cackling maws. Something tugged on her kimono and she looked down to see her grandfather, so tiny and vulnerable. Was he waiting to be swallowed up, too?

"Go." Ojiichan nodded up at her. "It's time."

"But…"

"I'm not hungry anymore," he repeated and smiled.

Okappa kicked off the claw-like hands of the neighbors she used to know that were clamping her ankles and raced to where the monkey lay crumpled and howling in a pile of red silk.

Hanshiro cursed and charged in her direction. He used his walking stick to beat at the creature surrounding him and clear his path.

"It'll be okay," Okappa noted the monkey's twisted ankle. The pain of it needled her heart. She felt it, too. She touched his forehead and he quieted. She knew what she had to do.

Okappa stepped on the rope that bound the god to this world and removed the sickle from her hip. With one swipe she sliced the tether in half.

"There," she said, wondering when was the last time the animal had been free.

She was about to replace the blade when something hit her hard on the back of the head and stars exploded behind her eyes. She dropped the tool and fell to one knee.

More jeering laughter, and this time voices she recognized. She looked up to see Fuhaku, his five brothers slapping him on the back and congratulating him on his aim. They all weighed a rock in their free hands and seemed to be debating whose turn it was to throw next.

Okappa scooped up the monkey and held him to her chest. She stood up on weak legs, her head throbbing. A line of wet trickled from her hairline down her spine.

Hanshiro broke through the beast and then stopped. A sudden blast of thunder tore the sky and rain began to spit down, popping the dirt.

"You have no idea what you've done, girl." The stranger began walking toward her again, slower this time.

"Here, let me help you." He held out one hand, palm open. His other hand gripped the walking stick, cocked behind him and ready to strike.

But it wasn't only the man who frightened Okappa. With every step he took in her direction, the beast closed in as well.

It was less human than before. Appendages were jointed at unnatural angles and covered in lengths of red-pebbled skin, sores full to bursting. Snarled locks of greasy hair grew too fast and snaked like vines, knotting together. Everywhere, the mouths' constant clacking and sucking of air through foul teeth and gums. The eyes, some angry, some sad, all of them blinking away sticky tears.

The beast was growing larger, and because of that the stage was just as quickly shrinking. There was nowhere to go.

The monkey clutched at her work kimono. Trembling, he weighed almost nothing in her arms. She held him closer and began backing away. She stumbled through the boxes and the stranger's bags until she bumped against the side of the well. Nowhere to go.

"Take me with you," she whispered into the animal's ear. "We don't belong here."

The rain fell harder now, but the shush of it still not loud enough to drown out the bellowing monster engulfing the makeshift stage.

Another rock flew and sliced her cheek. Okappa winced at the pain.

"Such a pretty, pretty girl." She heard Fuhaku boast to his brothers. He hurled another rock. "And so very, very cheap. You can buy her for the price of a stone."

"You know how this is going to end," Hanshiro said. The man was almost upon her. The sneer on his face confident he had won. His walking stick was gone and instead he was holding her sickle with both hands above his head.

Okappa climbed the stone wall of the well.

Her attention flitted past the stranger and the terrible thing the townspeople had become. There in the moment right before the beast attacked, right before Hanshiro reached her with his hatred and her blade, she saw her grandfather. The crooked curve of his back and the leaning way he had of walking. Her heart lightened. He was making his way in the opposite direction, past the crowd. He was going back home.

When her attention came back to the beast, it was too close. But worse was Hanshiro. He was right upon her, roaring and slashing down with the sickle.

Okappa twisted so that the knife missed the monkey at her breast and caught her arm and her side instead. The rip of cloth and her skin, cold and stinging underneath.

Hanshiro raised the weapon again. Nowhere to go. Okappa, holding the monkey close and whispering in his ear, turned and dove into the well.

They fell.

The rush of air sweet with the scent of dew and a mossy forest floor, trees, felt like it was slowing their descent.

The sweet wind whipped at her torn kimono. With the belt sliced through, the rough cloth opened and the sleeves released the tufts of crane down she'd collected all these years. The balls of fluff separating and floating around them like a pollen-filled sky.

It was growing darker. But not colder. Warmer.

The monkey chittered and wrapped his arms tighter around Okappa's neck. His silk robes flapped and slipped across her bare skin, silky gossamer licking her stomach, around her sides, caressing her back and her legs. She'd never felt anything so soft before.

She was finally leaving, she thought. They both were leaving. A syrupy poison softened her heart. For the first time since she could remember she was happy.

It was at that moment she realized they weren't falling at all.

They were soaring. They were flying up, up, up. The disc of black well water, rippling silver, turned a bright autumn-sky blue, and as they drew nearer it gained depth; no, height. The fragrance of crisp autumn leaves crushed underfoot, the sweet orangey perfume of *kinomokusei* blossoms filled her lungs.

On the edge of the new sky, she saw something stir. Something familiar. Her softened heart, too, then burst apart like the thousands of ethereal tufts of crane down dancing in the air around them.

Okappa smiled when she recognized what she saw. *Ichi, ni...* Just before they burst through the sky she watched a flock of cranes take wing. This time there were two more than this morning. Fledglings.

MAY BE DIM

Taro was as dim as he was huge. Three heads taller than everyone else, broad backed, sturdy waisted. He was useful despite his bum leg. Sometimes, on a dare, he would pick up the village horse—a small mangy thing with soft hooves and a nasty case of ringworm. So nasty, in fact, that not even the children risked petting it. But Taro didn't care. He hefted the animal up and counted to ten. He set it down. The wise ones clapped. The children squealed and fled and wouldn't play with him again until he bathed in the hottest of hot springs, until the wee ones deemed all the itchy bugs were gone. He did whatever he was told. Taro was useful.

In his thirteenth year he was given a very important job. Theirs was a small village, the soil too rocky, the weather too harsh. It was a community that could only support youth and those who gave back. They had learned before that their survival was owed to the wise ones' monthly council, to the decision whispered later into Taro's ear.

The day after the wise ones' gathering, Taro would kneel down on his good knee—the bad one stretched crooked at his side—and accept on his back whichever old man or woman could no longer contribute. He'd stand again, adjust his load, then plod along, rocking slightly, deep into the mountains. The only rule to this special task was that he come back alone.

The giant man may be dim but he was proud. And during the fifteen years of performing this onerous and quite dangerous work he had invented ways of making it easier. One thing he had learned was that it was best to keep the elderly person's mind occupied. Not to let them talk.

Once they started chattering they began to lament. Next came the begging, the weeping, and then the barrage of tiny enervated fists on the back of his head, tears and snot-drool down his neck. It was a situation best avoided.

Avoid it he did, by simply talking the entire journey.

Normally a silent man, this sudden verbosity always stunned the aging, mostly diseased—occasionally incontinent—villager. They listened to his stories, as if he had something important to say. He didn't really. He spun tales about where they were headed: Tobiori Falls, and about how it was the most beautiful place on earth, the closest to heaven, in fact. The easiest way to get there.

If he caught any feeling, however, the passenger preferred not to make the journey to the Other Side just yet, he'd prattle on about how once they arrived at the plateau, there was another choice. All they had to do was follow a narrow path that led to the opposite side of the mountain, to a town that actually revered their elderly. It was a half-day trek, he'd say, but if they chose to venture there, they would be rewarded in full. Taro would teach them the landmarks.

This was something else he had learned, another part of making the inevitable not so bad: a sliver of hope cured a lot of ills. After reaching the overhang he'd set his passenger under the gingko tree and point to the great open mouth of the chasm and, beyond that, the falls. If they were up to traveling the second path, he'd tell them what they needed to know for that choice.

While his doomed piggy-backer gaped in awe or shock, he'd press a rice ball into the pair of trembling hands, bow his goodbyes, and as quick as his feeble legs would let him, hurry back down the mountain pass. He needed to escape before the hungry ghosts realized someone was there.

The rumor only he was told was if a person stayed too long, the piles of weathered bones would begin to rattle and click; the wind that at first sounded like a woman's sigh through the trees would fall into a moan, rise into a screech. And the roar of the water in the ravine would be heard for what it really was: a thousand screaming souls. If he stayed too long, the village men warned, his feet would freeze to the ground as root-fingered hands assured he'd never make it home again. This was what happened to the man who did this job before him. And the man before that.

So far Taro had been lucky. He may be dim, but he was proud, and he was occasionally lucky.

Except for the disgruntled spirits part, it was a nice job. After his journey, safe in the village, Taro's heart still thumping in his chest and pain shooting up his leg and back, the villagers would all gather. The men sprinkled him with salt while the priests shook their beads and mumbled their sing-songy prayers. It was imperative to remove any sticky ghosts that might ride Taro back down the mountain. Then came the celebration. Food and drink until his belly was full to bursting and his head spun. It was the only time they allowed Taro to drink. It was the only time the entire town loved him completely. Life was good.

That is until the day he was approached by one of the wise ones and a too-familiar name was whispered in his ear. His own grandmother, his *Baaba*, the woman who had plucked him from a heap of smoldering refuse when, after his father's unfortunate accident, his mother ran off with a traveling soothsayer, depositing his little baby self on the garbage heap on her way out of town.

Taro inwardly grieved at the news but knew there was nothing he could do. Not just about the decision, but truly there was nothing else the large, awkward man could do. No other job in the village.

He was all but useless in the fields, and he wasn't agile enough with his fingers to weave sandals or straw raincoats. He had a propensity to daydream, which made him ill-suited for a job that required thinking. No, Taro had found that, while at times difficult, this line of work—bearing the weak into the hills—fit him perfectly. He may be dim, but he knew that if it wasn't for this he would be the least productive member of the village. Then he'd have to take himself up the mountain.

After the announcement, Taro retired to his shack on the outskirts of town and tried to rest. He wanted to be in top form for the journey, didn't want to trip over some stone or tree root and fall and injure his Baaba like that time with Ol' Jiro. Busted his arm up good, and oh, the wailing and sobbing he did the rest of the way up. Taro had a headache even the saké couldn't chase away.

He had barely gotten to sleep when he was suddenly woken from his nap by screeching and hoots of what sounded like joy. He hurried to the main street to find nearly all the villagers gathered in a circle, clapping and whistling and…laughing.

Taro always knew his Baaba was a very clever crone. But this time she had outdone herself. After hearing her fate she returned home and got to work. She washed her hair in squid's ink and donned the peach-colored kimono she had worn in her youth. Moth-eaten and several sizes too small, it didn't quite close in the front, but that didn't stop her from ambling about on fancy-cut geta and tittering behind the garment's long sleeves. The long sleeves announcing to all who observed that the wearer was an unmarried virgin. The town got a chuckle out of that. Her nine children shook their heads.

Out of pity, or the desperate need for entertainment, a new order was whispered to Taro. His Baaba had been granted a reprieve. It didn't take long for the other elderly in the village to figure out what she was doing. The idea spread. Grannies of all ages powdered their faces white and painted their lips into bright red bows. They wore their daughters' kimonos and sashayed down the streets giggling and flirting, very careful not to stumble and break a hip.

Meanwhile, once-crotchety old men, legs bowed and backs bent, slapped handfuls of damp kelp across their balding heads and began to frolic like spring foxes—decidedly slow and grunting spring foxes—as they attempted to raise kites or spin wooden tops with the village children. With so much effort it was difficult, when the moon grew full, to choose whose turn it was to Ride the Taro. Difficult but not impossible. The wise ones were wise. Every month another one went. But it was usually the least fancy, the least spritely of the bunch. His Baaba was safe.

But for how long he didn't know. As the days went by Taro noticed the wise ones moving through the village in packs. They mumbled amongst themselves, pointed at his Baaba, and nodded. Taro guessed they didn't find her cleverness as amusing as everyone else did. There was only one remedy for nails that stuck up.

Then it happened: a bad batch of quail eggs. Taro's grandmother woke up one morning with a wicked case of gas.

Which, naturally, she tried to blame on the stray dog that liked to sleep under the eave of her bedroom window. But the pain was intense. Groaning and clutching of the belly can easily be diagnosed as something contagious and deadly, in need of immediate attention. Attention she got.

The wise ones decided on a rush order. Disease must never be allowed to breed in the village. She must go, and right away. It took three men an hour and a half to load her onto her grandson's back. There was much flailing about and cursing, a handful of last trips to the bathroom and two near escapes.

During the last near escape, Taro hurried to his hut and made her a sticky rice ball, tucking in the biggest pickled plum he could find. He even made sure to remove the seed. He didn't want her to break a tooth. It was only last month he'd successfully delivered the village's only dentist to the falls.

Taro was clumping his way back to the village center when, distracted by the sight of his Baaba being carried his way, he tripped and landed hard on his knees. He pushed himself to his feet and was about to toss the stick that had tangled in his legs when he noticed something in the swirl of the grain and the knotty twists in the wood.

It looked exactly like a Buddha seated in meditation. Maybe not a perfect Buddha, one shoulder was hitched higher than the other, and the eyes weren't exactly symmetrical, one of the arms ended at the elbow, but this was most certainly a Buddha. It was an auspicious sign.

Taro slipped the lucky Buddha stick into his sleeve and waited for his Baaba to be brought to him. She had managed to make it all the way to her home this last time and was changed into her favorite kimono. Threadbare now, it still held the vibrant persimmon color that brought out the blush in her cheeks. She'd also refreshed her makeup and oiled her hair.

Exhausted, no doubt, the old woman seemed to finally accept her sentence and let herself be loaded onto Taro's waiting back. She slumped against him, quiet and hot and damp from exertion. Her long, tied up hair smelled of camellias. It reminded him of his youth, when she wore the scent daily.

Taro bowed his head to the crowd and set off. He was grateful that his Baaba immediately fell into a deep sleep. He didn't feel like conversation at all. He especially didn't feel like telling his hopeful story about the secret path. The story that didn't have any truth to it at all.

Instead he concentrated on each rocking footstep, one after the other, careful so the gravel didn't roll from under his sandals—especially the one with the thicker sole—and pull his weak leg out from under him. He'd already fallen once today. His only urgent thought was that he wished he could have left the village earlier.

Maybe it was the stillness of his little old granny on his back snoring like a hornet, or maybe it was the way the shadows grew sinister as the sun dissolved into a deeper and deeper orange. Tonight they seemed more agitated than usual. Either way, the journey took way too long.

By the time he reached the clearing, the moon had already risen. It wasn't quite full but enough to bathe everything in a swimmy underwater blue. Taro limped to the gnarled tree that stood at the edge of the cliff and gently laid his grandmother down. Now when she woke up she'd be facing the magnificent Tobiori Falls.

He swung his sleeves. One held the lucky Buddha stick, the other the leaf-wrapped rice ball. He was about to retrieve the meal to place in her hands when a quick gust of wind swept leaves across the clearing, making a hollow clicking sound, like someone fast approaching.

Taro whipped his head around. No one. He took a moment to gaze at the thousands of pale bones strewn about; on some, meat still clung, hair and clothes. The dentist, near whole, was crumpled where Taro had last seen him, praying to his own Buddha that would never arrive in time. Taro wondered when things would begin to move. Maybe the village men had just been teasing him all along. He didn't want to stay and find out.

Taro was lumbering away when he heard someone call his name.

"Taro," the voice said. "We need to talk."

He jumped and turned. It was his Baaba. She was standing at the edge of the ravine with her back to him, gazing at the cascades below, moon reflecting, backlighting. She looked like the ghost she hadn't yet become. Taro was proud. She'd be a very elegant ghost.

A sudden scattering of chill bumps prickled his neck when he realized that he had never witnessed such clear-headedness after one of her naps. It became real to him that she had probably been awake the entire journey up.

"Do you remember when you were a child?" She turned around to face him.

"*Hai*," Taro answered.

"I'm sure you don't remember how I saved you as a baby. How I pulled the rats off your leg and one by one crushed them with a rock."

Taro's stomach twisted. Was this the truth? He rubbed his throbbing thigh, down to his calf. He had always been told this was a birth defect; it was why his mother didn't take him with her. If that was the case, he could forgive her. But was it a lie? Had he once been whole?

"No," Taro said. "I don't remember."

"But you do remember how everyone taunted you? How you couldn't walk until you were almost six and how even doctor Hanjiro and the head monk of the temple were at a loss for what to do?"

Taro remembered that.

"Did you know it was me who asked the geta maker to place the extra wedge of wood on the bottom of your right shoe so you could walk more evenly?"

Heat rose in Taro's face. It was true. It wasn't until that shoe that he was able to stump along, build some strength in his bad leg. The villagers enjoyed watching him fumble and fall. They asked him to run this way and that. But all those silly errands were what made him strong. That and the special shoe. It's what made him the man he was now.

"This is my job. It's very important. I've lasted longer than all the others. I can't let them down," Taro said. He hoped she could understand.

Instead the old woman let out a horrible cry, ripped at her hair, and dropped to all fours. She thrashed about. "I should just throw myself over and be done with it."

"No!" Taro shouted. She stopped and looked up at him. He considered telling her the lie about the path that led to a freer and more tolerant town, but changed his mind.

"Why not? It's the same thing," she said.

It wasn't the same thing. There were two types of ghosts that haunted this spot. There were the ones that arrived after he'd left someone sitting under the old tree, a pat on the head and some food in their hands. Oh, they might grow angry. But not always at him. More often than not they understood the cycle of things. If anything they were sad that they hadn't been given a little more time, or perhaps grateful that he'd delivered them to such a beautiful place.

Suicides, however, were different. They were angry at a higher level, a sharper, more directed hate. The wrath of someone who took her own life would follow a man around, get inside his head, and he'd never be right again. Salt didn't remove those.

"Please...," Taro said.

The old woman crawled backward until the toes of one sandaled foot dangled over the edge.

"Do you think this is any worse than you leaving me here for the animals? Do you think I'd rather my skin be stripped by foxes and bones broken by wild boars?"

She had a point. Taro moved closer. He got within three strides of her when she shifted, threatening again to plunge herself over the side. He halted and eased down to his aching, skinned knees. He sat back on his heels. As much as he could, he straightened his back—muscles knotting in his hips and down the side of his bad leg. This was the most polite way to sit. This would show that what he was going to say was from his heart. She had to listen. The pain in his leg and side moved to a shimmery numbness. Taro prostrated himself, forehead rubbing gravel, before sitting up straight again.

"Baaba, I implore you."

She looked up at him, trembling, tiny. The nightingale dung she'd used to whiten her face was melting down her cheeks and neck, leaving her real skin an awful gray color. The madder she'd used to redden her lips had smeared on one side all the way to her ear, so it looked as if she was half smiling at him. Then there was her hair—haloed by watery moonlight. It was pulled so completely from its chignon that it fell wild and brittle-dry all the way to the ground. To Taro it resembled the long untamed mane of the little soft-hoofed horse he liked to carry around.

The thought spurred another memory: how when he was very small his grandmother used to ride him on her back like a horse.

Her own children, his aunts and uncles, wouldn't play with him at all. It was his Baaba who would chase them out of the house and stay with Taro on her hands and knees, bucking and whinnying, and pawing at the straw matted floor with her knuckles still raw from working in the fields.

Taro's heart moved. This woman had sacrificed so much for him. It was true. Without her he'd be a handful of ash. She took him in, fed him, fought for him. She was the only one never to have teased him. She loved him. He loved her.

"You're right," Taro said and held out his arms. "I can't leave you."

This is how he'd do it: he'd explain to the villagers that he now intended to share his meals with his old grandmother, that, also, she could move in with him. She wouldn't be a burden to anyone at all. He'd take care of his Baaba the way she'd taken care of him. When it was her time to go, he would be by her side. This was the way it should be. Taro felt light and giddy inside. This was the first big decision he'd ever made by himself. This is what being a man meant. Suddenly there was no doubt in his mind. He had the energy to trek back down the mountain even with his Baaba on his back.

He was about to speak when someone whispered near his ear, close, giggling, far away. An uneven cut of a fingernail slid across his cheek, pinched the skin of his neck. Taro jumped and a pile of bones that he hadn't noticed had been stacked so high clattered to the ground at his side.

"We have to hurry," he said.

There was only a moment's hesitation before his grandmother understood she had won. She was going home. Delight lit up her face.

"Taro-bo!" She pushed herself to her feet and extended her own arms to her grandson.

Around them the whisperings grew louder, so that now they could be heard even over the roar of the falls.

There was the distinct click and crunch of footfalls on dry, dusty bone.

"We need to leave now." Something moved out of the corner of Taro's eye, the swish of a silk kimono in the tall grass. He felt presences moving in. Hundreds of them. He'd stayed too long.

Taro leapt to his feet. Only it had been a long hike and a long time kneeling. There was his bad leg. He took a step to retrieve his grandmother, but something was wrong. It felt like a dozen sets of teeth gnawing up and down the soft parts of his legs. Numb. And then there came a stifled laugh and what might have been the sudden thrust of a fist into the small of his back. Taro was a big man. His tall form falling, hands outstretched, he hit his sweet smiling grandmother hard just above the knees. He tried to grab at her and missed. A piece of cloth tore away.

Right before she disappeared over the edge, he saw the glint of hope in her teary eyes quickly change to surprise and then terror as she realized the big brute hurtling toward her wasn't going to stop, and he wasn't going to catch her either.

Gone.

Taro swallowed.

Alone.

The chattering forest fell dead quiet. Taro rolled over and tested the strength of his legs, massaged his thigh and back. He got up again, gutted, confused. He glanced around the clearing expecting his dear old Baaba to pop out from behind a rock or a

shadowy pile of bones. But she didn't. Here it was again, Taro's fault. He was dim and clumsy and unlucky. He shook his head. No, no, no. He opened his clenched fist and saw a length of persimmon-colored cloth, ripped from the *okumi*-hem of his Baaba's favorite kimono.

Yes.

After a moment's thought, Taro tied the cloth around his wrist. There was no other choice, nothing else he could do. He brushed the dirt from his clothes, turned, and began his journey down the mountain. Slow and rocking, he concentrated on one step at a time.

Behind him the wind in the trees picked up and it almost sounded like a spattering of laughter and polite applause. That's what he was returning to. That was the happy reception he'd get when he arrived back in the village so long after dark. No one had ever made it home at this late hour before. He would be the first to survive such a dangerous journey, and with a story to tell, too. He'd be a hero.

A weight in his sleeve caught his attention. Taro stuck his hand in and discovered the hastily made sticky rice ball. Maybe he wasn't so unlucky after all. He felt the other sleeve for his Buddha stick. Still there. Another good sign.

113

He peeled back the leaves on the rice ball and took a bite. The flavor of sour plum exploded in his mouth and tightened his cheeks. He smiled as he imagined the villagers slapping him on the shoulders and telling him what a good job he'd done. His heart flew. He was never happier than when he had a cup pressed to his lips, saké chilling and then numbing his tongue and throat, heating his belly. Drink more! *Yoku gambatta!*

Taro had an idea. Tonight after the celebrations and the salt-sprinkled shoulders, he'd tell the story of his grandmother's unfortunate and sudden demise. Then tomorrow, while battling his usual dry headache, he would build an altar in the corner of his hut for his dear Baaba.

Taro would then decorate this *butsudan* with the lucky Buddha stick. He'd drape the torn piece of kimono around the uneven shoulders, and arrange a spray of flowers in an unused cup. He'd do more. Every day he'd burn incense and leave a small plate of rice for her ghost to nibble. He'd pray.

Since nothing was ever secret in his village for long, everyone would soon notice what he'd done. They'd praise him for his filial piety and thank him for keeping her surely nettled spirit appeased.

It wouldn't be difficult after that for him to suggest he be given a bottle of saké to further pacify her ghost. An *ochoko* cup offered at the feet of the Buddha stick every morning would surely do the trick. Maybe he could offer a cup at night, as well.

Taro's mouth watered at the thought. He smacked his lips. He may be dim, but sometimes he was very, very smart.

THE UN-HARMONIOUS MAN

One

Sora wakes with a gasp and starts gulping for air.

"Everything's going to be okay." A familiar hand squeezes her shoulder, the shoulder that is nailed to the trunk of an enormous persimmon tree.

Sora can't move her head either. It's secured to the wood, but she doesn't yet know how. Probably tied. She only learned about the foot-long nail angled sideways under her clavicle last week. She was trying to focus through the pus-film that pooled in her eyes, when she noticed the knobby end of a spike, the long shaft bent. Her only thought at the time and since was had it been an old spike going in, or had it been hammered and re-hammered so often and so hard that the metal had aged and weakened. She couldn't remember how long she'd been like this.

"I'm here to help you," He says.

Sora pulls a stiff smile. It doesn't hurt anymore. As long as she doesn't move, that is. She feels she should be grateful for that. So many people suffer in this world. But not her. Days slip by easier this way, and there is always some tiny kindness to cling to. Like the trembling beastie she knows is shying in the shadow-cup of a broken branch cavity nearby.

It will wait until He leaves, and then appear gray-furred and mercury-eyed in the moonlight to chitter and hum and try to untangle her hair with its needle claws. It will call its friends with a lilting whistle, and they will all spend the lengthy night huddled together. Sora wishes she could pet them, but even her arms are impaled.

So with the tang of musk rubbing her skin and spinning her thoughts, she'll sing little songs to let the creatures know how much she loves them and appreciates them. She'll grow warm and for one more night none of them will be alone.

Another kindness right now, mitigating the papery twist-nag of hunger in her belly: His words.

"I'm going to get help. I'm going to save you," He says. He takes the cuff of His sleeve and dabs at her streaming eyes. Her vision clears, and she sees He doesn't frown or look repulsed or wipe the soiled shirt on the bark by her head.

The corners of His eyes curl; the uneven horns creak and jut a little farther from His leathery forehead. He's happy, she thinks. He loves her. In all this time, long or short—she doesn't know for sure—He's never returned with any help.

"Thank you," Sora says and lets herself be kissed. The bite of something viscous and sleepy wells up on the fat of His tongue and fills her mouth and throat. For the moment her hunger abates. Things aren't so bad.

As He feeds, Sora closes her newly cleared eyes and escapes to yesterday when, while alone, she caught sight of that frequently appearing shape lurching about the field in front of her. She spends far too much time fretting over the strange man. But what else is there to do?

She sometimes tries to remember when she first noticed him and when she first figured out something was wrong. He isn't like anyone else she's ever met or seen, not like the constant Him who cares for her.

There is a way things are done here, and the man who spends all day in the field doesn't quite belong. He moves in a different rhythm than this world, out of sync and intermittent. Sora, on the other hand, prides herself on fitting in so completely. The unharmonious man, however, doesn't seem to follow these same rules. It has always bothered her.

Recently though something changed, and it was only yesterday when she realized what nightmarish things he was doing. She could tell from the screams on the wind and from his big, discordant movements she caught through her squinted eyes. Sunlight crackled the blur just enough to ensure there was no doubt. A rage she'd never felt before shook her. Teeth against teeth, and she blinked to clear the black that smoked her eyes. Sora tried to call out to him, to tell him to stop torturing the beasties, to stop hurting them, to leave them alone.

But that thing that erupts when she's afraid started filling her guts and foaming her mouth until her voice was stifled again. Somehow she had to get his attention and let him know she was angry.

Sora had an idea. She dug the toes of one bare foot into the dirt, the ball of the other she braced against the lump of an exposed root. She sucked air through her teeth and as hard as she could she pushed. Her knotted hair and the spike pinning her shoulder loosened a little, but the stakes she didn't know about—the one piercing her hip, and another driven into the thick of her thigh—grabbed and held tight. She cried out with a voice that for an instant dissolved the thing that always silenced her. It was a voice louder than she knew she had. It hurt, but this time in a good way.

The un-harmonious man looked over and waved his arm high overhead. It's what he did. He reached down and seized another beastie and flung it across the field. Sora had to escape. She had to stop him.

Another attempt to propel herself forward shot the pain through a spider net and straight up her spine. Instant-black inked her eyes and Sora fell limp against the stakes and wept. She gave up. And for the first time in as long as she could remember she hated herself for doing so.

Two

The moon ticks its measured descent. The sky around it ripples watery blue, then black.

He never comes at this hour. He never has. Usually she's asleep or in braided thoughts with her beasties, but not tonight. Tonight she strains her neck and uses her teeth to gather up the loose cloth that drapes her shoulder. She fills her mouth and bites down hard.

Tears in her eyes, she presses the back of her head against the tree and searches inside herself for something that could constitute strength. It might be a memory. She grunts a count to three and, with every bit of strength she has, snaps her head forward as far as she can. Pain explodes; the tangled and tied hair loosens just a little bit more. An arm is almost free.

Sora falls back, breathing hard. She whimpers, but before fear can freeze her, she begins hunting for what will spur her next effort.

A finger of blood trickles down her forehead and catches in her eyebrow. The beastie latched to the trunk near her head stretches over and laps at it with its wormy tongue. When she starts to shiver, another creature clambers up her side and hums the song she so often sings to them. It's a hopeful song. It's her idea of what a love song should be. The beastie then uses the pads of two fingers to press and massage her ear. Its whiskers tremble. Its teeth click.

Each attempt at breaking free is getting harder and harder,

and Sora doesn't know how long she can go on. Already the world is starting to pink. She's not sure when He'll arrive. It's been awhile since He's abandoned her for days. Is He due? But Sora can't judge. She can never judge.

She remembers the time He left for a month and shudders. Thirty days notched into the bark with her fingernails. When he returned he said he liked it better when she is hungry. She's more grateful. It's more attractive.

Sora has to believe she has more time.

Above her the curling autumn-dry leaves rattle. Sora's never really looked at the tree that surrounds her against a blushing sky. But now that she has a little movement in her head she does. It's a hand, she thinks, a many, broken-fingered hand, thrusting from the earth and clutching at her.

Overhead a shadow leaps heavy from branch to branch. A brittle snap and it descends again. Sora jumps as the ripped flesh of a persimmon fruit is pushed up against her lips. She opens her mouth and chews. Overripe and jelly-like between her teeth, the mealy sweetness pinches her cheeks and fills her. She eats torn piece after piece.

"Thank you," Sora whispers when the beastie plucks the last smooth seed from her mouth and cracks it between its own teeth.

Sora nods the creatures away and without any count at all jerks forward again and again and again.

Three

Now the day is warm, the sun having ballooned the sky and painted it porcelain blue.

Sora limps across the field, her right foot falling crooked, wrong. The pain, a screwing sensation, drills up her leg with every step. There's the headache that flutters and cuts. There's the weeping flesh of her thigh from the single barbed spike she didn't know about until too late. And right there in her chest, as exposed as the world around her, knocks an anticipative hollow, an elation.

This is the first time she's been off the tree. She staggers forward, trying to get as much distance as she can between her and the imprisoning fist. Her and Him. The scent of clover and rapeseed blossoms fill her head and spark emotions she can't identify. The early morning insects trill like hidden treasures buried all about her feet.

A single sob overcomes her as she recalls a false memory of her as a child playing in this very field. She was whole then. She was happy. The memory, though, is a fairy tale she has told herself repeatedly throughout the years. It is where she goes when it becomes too much. It never really happened.

She looks up and that's when she sees him. The un-harmonious man is standing backlit on the crest of a low hillock in the distance, unmoving. He's not taunting the beasties. Not waving. This new inaction frightens Sora. He's bigger than she imagined. More real. Suddenly she's not sure about her choice.

She glances back over her shoulder and wonders when He will return. He'll come with a meal and words she's heard a thousand times before. He'll wipe her sores and curl his smile and ignore her for the rest of the day. With the thought comes the reek of sour alcohol-hiss on his breath and the way her stomach will knot and tremble. A clammy hand reaches up and grabs her throat.

Sora turns once more to face the stranger. Still too far away to judge or understand. He's framed in nothing but open space. There is nowhere to hide. But she is curious. All fear is black, but this one she's willing to enter.

Sora continues her broken pace. The un-harmonious man still hasn't moved. As she gets closer she sees he's shirtless, bearded. Some of her beasties spring away from her and gather at his feet. They're too trusting, she thinks. She needs to reach them before they are hurt or worse.

"Stop," she says, her voice strangled small in her mouth.

The uneven earth tests her balance with each rocking step, meadow grasses tickle her legs, and the rising sun sears her vision gold. A veil slips away. She senses she might recognize this man after all, like he's a memory she's always known. Sora understands now with the same ballooning elation that filled the sky that she is wrong about her earlier recollection. This isn't the first time she's been off the tree.

She stops. Two more steps and she could touch him.

The un-harmonious man is tall and thin. His eye color is wrong, a color she's never seen in eyes before. There are no horns. No claw-like teeth. His skin isn't perfect leather. And there, snaking down his chest and stomach, a raised scar as if something in life has torn him open. She wonders if he's some kind of monster. She wonders if he has escaped his own tree.

Sora holds his stare and squares her shoulders. She lengthens her spine. She needs to look strong and intimidating. She squeezes tight the one spike she kept from her hell. It's the longest one, the barbed one. The metal has gone hot in her grip. She has to tell this man exactly what she thinks. Show him.

He stares and for the first time a spasm of embarrassment runs through her. She knows what she must look like. Dirtied, bloodied, broken. She brushes the thought away and adjusts her frock with her free hand. No matter what she wears, it will never look right; the way the cloth will cling flat to where He cleaved her right breast so many years ago.

Just then a beastie comes bounding up from behind the stranger. It leaps. The un-harmonious man twists, his arm shoots out, and he catches it. Before Sora can even protest, he spins once and launches it into the air.

"No!" This time her voice has weight.

The man turns back to her. But Sora watches in horror as the beastie screams a high-pitched sound. It stretches out webbed arms and legs, glides, and then makes a safe, if clumsy, landing. There is a yowl and then an excited chittering as it finds its feet and comes romping back to the un-harmonious man's side.

She doesn't understand.

The beastie that was riding on her hip squeaks, drops to the ground, and jumps into the stranger's arms.

"Don't hurt it," Sora pleads.

"Hurt it?" The man cocks his head and lifts the creature to perch on his shoulder where it nuzzles his hair and purrs. The un-harmonious man laughs.

At first it sounds like teasing and Sora is angry again, but the longer she listens she hears it's only laughing, and the beasties gathering in the field are thrilling at the sound of it. There are so many more than she imagined.

"Do they belong to you?" she asks.

"The little ones? No. I help them. They help me. We play."

Play. That is another thing Sora has forgotten. But it comes back to her now and unsteadies her feet. She's suddenly in the same field with her best friend racing beside her. They're screaming childhood pleas of protection into the quick gusts of wind that steal their voices and smother them dead.

They hope one prayer will reach the heavens and save them, because right now, at their backs, an indigo cloudbank closes in. The rain sheets white and gray and hisses like fire eating the dry grass. It's moving faster than they are. When a belly-growl of thunder erupts above, Sora squeals and yells over her shoulder for the monster that is going to devour them to stay away. The two children continue their flight terrified and happy. They're laughing.

"I try to care for them at night," Sora says. She's back in the real world. The beasties continue to gather.

"Yes, I send them. They tell me all about you," he pauses.

Something crosses his face before he speaks again. "You're free now."

Sora has always had vivid dreams. When her life plummets into the unbearable, those dreams are more real and hold her faster than her waking. She suddenly worries this field, this man, this baking sun on her face are all one of those dreams. It was so bad before she escaped the tree. Maybe, any second now, He'll shake her awake, slap her face.

She wants to thank the un-harmonious man. She doesn't know how. Sora takes a step forward. She reaches out and touches his scar. He shivers. She runs two fingers down the curve. She can feel him looking at her and she thinks he's going to back away. He's going to disappear again. He always leaves her.

She remembers all those days before now, and how she looked forward to the time he'd appear, slow and methodical over the rise. She'd study him, straining to focus, until she was sure she knew everything about him. Later she'd watch him stand to face the persimmon tree. Her.

She guessed the setting sun at her back was magnificent. She'd never seen it. She didn't know. Then, while there was still enough light for her to make out his dark form, he'd turn and walk away and vanish behind the low hill.

Right now his skin burns under her fingers, but he doesn't flee. Not this time. Instead the stranger places the palm of his hand against the flat of her chest and waits for her heart to start beating again.

"You're okay," he says. "All of you."

She believes him like she's never believed anyone before. She's going to cry. To stop herself she shifts her attention down the hill behind the man. There sits a small hut with a thatched roof. The windows and front door are thrown open. A single shirt is drying on a line. She always imagined the un-harmonious man coming from so much farther away.

That's when she sees it. There is a boulder and in it a stake driven to the hilt. From the fat metal curl at the end, a chain stretches across the ground toward her. The links pulled taut end at the crest of the hill, at the shackle cuffing the un-harmonious man's calf. He notices her reaction and takes a step back.

Sora doesn't hesitate. She moves forward and kneels. She lifts the spike she saved from the prison-tree with both hands and brings it down on the shackles over and over. The beasties squeak and back away, but she keeps stabbing at the shackles until her palms run bloody and the metal finally snaps.

The un-harmonious man helps her to her feet. With trembling hands he pulls her close. She wraps her arms around his waist and fills the hollow of his missing ribs. Her head puzzles into the space where the side of his chest concaves. His skin smells like rain and summer grass and memories.

Sora looks out past the hut. She blinks and for the first time in years her vision goes absolutely clear. She gasps. Until right now she used to think the horizon was the hill the man crested every day. She was wrong. The land stretches forever, dipping and rising. Fields are squared with low stone walls, and trees of the most verdant green stand all about in clusters or alone. Not a single one looks like a clutching hand. There are no prisoners that she can see. Her gaze follows a river that shimmers and narrows as it snakes away into a distant tree line. Mountains.

"I think I'm going to go that way." She points.

"You know, I've always wondered about that way myself," he says. "I've never been."

He kisses her on the top of the head, and he ruffles her hair. They begin to walk together.

"I used to dream about you," he says.

Sora briefly worries again that this is one of her own overly lucid dreams. But it can't be. There is something different. It takes her a few seconds—a few plodding steps—before she understands. The difference is it isn't as perfect as in her dreams. Her dreams are flawless. But now she's very much afraid. But mixed with the fear she feels confident and curious and free, a hundred other things, both good and bad. This is going to be hard, she knows, but she wants to do this. This time it's her decision.

The sun burns its way up the sky and is now almost directly overhead as the two falter forward, at turns leaning into each other and standing straight and separate again. Behind them a thatched-roof hut rests empty, a giant persimmon tree grows smaller, less daunting, and hundreds of glossy-eyed beasties coo and whistle and chitter as they follow, scampering through the grasses at the couple's heels.

Sora smiles at them and then up at the un-harmonious man. Her eyes cloud again, but the tears spill and the scenery before them sparkles. Her chest grows warm and she sings her song.

MY DOG BUCKY

"Don't do it, man." Toby, the bass player in our punk band The Penetralia, blew himself a many-tentacled, strawberry-scented vape beard then shook it off. "Not only is it a dumb idea, it's a dick thing to do."

"Naw, naw, it's okay," I said. "It'll be funny. Besides, you've seen him. You know what I'm talking about. Total spaz. If the dude's going to play with us, he's gotta chill."

I was right, you know. We needed him and we needed him bad. We also needed him to be a little more punk and a lot less Ron Weasely. And don't get me started on the jumpsuit, all silver sparkly and shit. I don't know what active polymers and titanium dioxide nanotubes are, but that shit was lame.

The thing was, we had just scored our first gig at The Kraken, opening for the legendary band My Dog Bucky. I know, I know. Dream come true, right?

Only I had it on good authority we only got the spot because we had the hottest Theremin player in town. Well, he was the hottest until last month—while blazing through a particularly lusty version of "Everything Sucks," he slipped on some leftover spooge, fell head over heels, and broke all four fingers on his pitch control hand. Ever see one of those things played by a guy wearing a cast? Not. Cool.

So that's when I did what any proactive punk rocker does: I scoured Craig's List. There he was, Creeter, a self-professed Theremin god. Dude even had himself a three-radio Theremin. YouTube videos were out of this world. Hells yeah, I thought.

But when he showed up at practice, he was all squirrelly, had a big pair of BCGs that kept slipping down his nose. And that jumpsuit, right? That's when I got the idea. Little Ol' Creeter needed a little ol' dose of Toby's Special-T, Super Mellow.

Toby is a man of two talents. I tell you, if he wasn't the best bassist in the University District he'd make his fortune on his tailored-for-your-mood pot brownies. Okay, there's a lot more than pot in there, but who am I to judge. Those puppies are sweet. Sweet, get it?

The night before the big gig, the band holed up in my grandma's basement, doing a final run through of our set list, sucking down PBRs, and noshing on Toby's brownies. The idea was just to get Creeter chillaxed and maybe into a pair of black jeans and a Ramones tee. But an hour in and the kid started to freak out.

Next thing we know he's slapping at those big pockets he's got sewed all over his metallic overalls, wiping and rewiping his Coke-bottle lenses, and talking into that goofy bracelet watch that snakes all the way up to his elbow. He's all, "Come in, come in, can you hear me," and we're all rolling on the floor, grabbing our guts and howling.

In retrospect, I should have let him go right then and there. But, again, the kid had talent, and this was our big break. Anyone would have made the same mistake, right?

The night of the show, a line stretched out the door all the way to Bahn Mi'. The joint was packed and the band jacked. Creeter, while not exactly chill, wasn't his usual über-geek self either. He seemed serious, kept checking and rechecking the dials on his Theremin, mumbling to himself and adjusting the belt on his jumpsuit.

Then the lights went down and we were up. The first two songs were sick. We played our crowd favorites—"Bleed the Worm" and "Jenny-Crack Diet." By the time we dove into our version of "Holiday in Cambodia" I saw the mates from My Dog Bucky drop their quarters on the pinball machine and saunter over to hear us play. Dream come true, man, dream come true. Next we slid into our fourth number, a dark, spooky piece called "Sowers of Grief."

This was Creeter's moment to shine, his twenty-minute solo. But something wasn't right. To start with, he was all out of tune, warbly, and not in a good way, and then it was like someone threw a switch.

The kid flipped the fuck out. He revved the Theremin up a half-dozen octaves, turned the volume to eleven, and started scratching at the air like he was having a fit. Girls yowled and pawed at their ears. Guys hawked loogies all over his silver—I'd dare say it was glowing—spacesuit.

The band stopped playing, and I'm yelling over the wailing machine for him to chill the hell out, and still Creeter's center stage, spazzing and flapping his arms. That's when it happened. He reached over and snapped off the antenna to his machine and started slashing it around.

"Corrections must be made!" he screamed and swung the thing at the line of people closest to the stage. Sliced a burly, tattooed punk right across the forehead. A quick sheet of blood down the face and the big guy dropped. "The present must be changed!"

The band and me, we knew this wasn't going to end well. I dropped my ax, Toby his Fender P, even our drummer—whose name I can never remember and who is usually so lit he can't find his way off the stage after the show—was hurdling the cowering crowd to get out of there.

I don't know. Maybe we should have warned the others, dragged a couple with us, especially the lead singer for My Dog Bucky. I loved that guy. A saint. I looked back over my shoulder as I ducked out the front door and saw Creeter frothing at the mouth, holding the antenna all reverse-grip overhead and stabbing the hell out of anyone in his way.

"I do this to save the future!" he kept saying over and over, breathing hard. "Please understand."

Boom, stab, down. The last thing I saw right before I bolted down the street was the lead singer for My Dog Bucky get it right through the neck. Arterial blood stream, for the win. Damn. And the whole time, behind all the screaming and mayhem, the crazy Theremin was howling as if it had a life of its own, as if it was sadly lamenting the demise of every last person in the bar. Or, I don't know, maybe Creeter was right; maybe it was somehow singing us a brighter future.

THE CARP-FACED BOY

Horse and Bones—

Grandpa Tetsu squatted behind the rustling curtain of a willow tree, his near-crippled hands weaving horseshoes from lengths of stiff straw. With the completion and knotting off of each row, he squinted over at the one-storied, thatched-roof house—paper windows and doors thrown open to catch the breeze—to check if his family was sneaking up on him again. He needed to keep his distance, especially now that his daughter had returned; and she wasn't alone.

For weeks he'd been battling a thorny ache inside his chest. It felt like the deep end of hunger, or possibly a warning. And then two nights ago, through the sheeting rain, he heard the neighing of a pained horse and with it a baleful cautioning only his keen ears could detect. He let his wife welcome his daughter and her son—the most unwelcome of guests—while he fell back asleep certain that something very, very bad was going to happen soon.

There was the sound of feet slapping wooden floors, but still no one came outside. The horse beside him shifted uncomfortably on its spongy hooves, and Grandpa Tetsu reached up and patted its ribbed belly. What kind of monster rode a limping horse all the way from the city in the pouring rain until its shoes tattered and fell off?

The old man stood, balancing himself with one hand on the animal's sunken back. He stretched and slapped at the kinks in his crickety legs. Used to be he could stand most hours of the day, walk to Takakusa Mountain and back, and never tire. But that was a long time ago. He retrieved his wife's tortoiseshell comb from his sleeve and carefully began working the knots out of the creature's matted mane.

"Good boy." Grandpa Tetsu inhaled the dusty, sweaty-warm odor of the animal and the knot in his chest eased. "At least she brought you."

The shrill scream of a child came from the direction of the house. Movement and laughter. The old man ducked. He watched as his wife and daughter burst from the open door and marched over. They planted their baskets of laundry not more than a stone's throw away from where he stood crouching behind the horse's nervous legs. Not noticing him, the two began pulling water from the well. The child, strapped to his mother's back with long pieces of soft cloth, squirmed and kicked his chubby legs. It looked as if he might be in pain. Or possessed. The thought lingered a little too long, and almost as if he'd heard it, the boy stopped, turned, and looked directly at his grandfather. Something poisonous passed between them. Grandpa Tetsu shuddered and fell back against the tree.

He'd been seen by the carp-faced boy.

It was unnerving: eyes goggling, startled wide; long, wet lashes. Grandpa Tetsu had never seen the child blink. Not ever. That must mean something. Then there was the mouth, thick lipped and down turned, every now and then popping open in that desperate famished way of the candy-colored carp in the pond. When he first saw the child last spring, the old man had expected him to speak, to form a sentence or two, to say something frightful or wise. But no, instead, from the empty cavity spilled only a long line of drool or, when disgruntled, the occasional howl. An ear-splitting, unnatural cry that continued until those heavy sagging cheeks splotched red and a more awful-colored substance oozed from his nose. Something about the child was all wrong.

In an effort to stay calm, the old man pulled loose the pouch tied around his waist and placed it on the ground between his legs. He wriggled his entire fist inside, retrieved a handful of fish bones, and stuffed them into his mouth. Slowly he chewed. The briny-salt taste tightened his cheeks and jaw. His appetite flared. Fat, fish-faced child, he thought, leaning forward, daring another

136

look. The boy continued to stare, turning his head every time his mother moved so as not to lose sight of the old man. What was he thinking? After a moment, the toddler's thick arm flailed and steadied, pointing in his direction. An icy claw gripped the back of Grandpa Tetsu's neck and he pushed himself flat against the tree once more.

And why was he so fat anyway? When the entire town was fighting to put something in their belly, what was that ugly boy feasting on? Grandpa Tetsu filled his mouth with more bones. Worked them angrily between his jaws.

"When all I have to eat are these." But with the mumbled words his mood lightened slightly.

It was his best-kept secret. Grandpa Tetsu was the town's elder. Old and healthy, he was revered for his exceptional luck. During his entire life he'd not so much as suffered a broken bone, even that time he fell off the roof last winter and landed on his head. The most remarkable thing, though, was the fact that he had never lost a tooth. Everyone else his age spent meals mashing watery sweet potatoes between tender gums. Not Grandpa Tetsu. Almost daily townspeople stopped by to discuss the weather and ask his advice on health and long life. And almost daily Grandpa Tetsu told them lies.

He thought that telling the truth lessened its power. So the paper seller with the persistent cough was told to stir cicada husks into his morning soup, and the *geta* maker's wife with the full-body rash was instructed to make a tincture of the lizard's tail plant and early morning dew and apply it to the infected areas.

Strangely, most of the remedies worked.

His real secret, though, was fish bones. Collected from the garbage after meals and roasted a second time over warm coals until they cracked and blackened. He sprinkled them with sea salt and kept them in a cloth bag around his waist. He ate them whenever the hunger pangs came. Which very often occurred in the middle of the night. The thought of nighttime led his thoughts to what happened the previous one—when his daughter and only grandchild slept under the same roof.

A sound? A weight on his chest? He had bolted upright, blinking in the dusky glow of the *andon* lamp, puzzling at what had woken him so suddenly. He listened hard expecting another warning, but heard only the whirr of insects and the erratic dry snore of his wife in the next futon. There was a draft, so he turned, his eyes adjusting to the gloom. There he saw the bedroom door pushed open, and sitting in the hall, skin dyed orange and jumpy by the oil lamp, leaking piteously from an open mouth: the carp-faced boy. At the memory, Grandpa Tetsu's mood returned to its recent sour state.

"Horsey!"

Grandpa Tetsu jumped, scratching his back against the rough bark of the tree, his feet kicking the half-made horseshoes and his bag of fish bones. There under the horse's chest the child wobbled on his grotesque legs, his curious eyes, his mouth turned into a fishhook smile.

Grandpa Tetsu's wife laughed and trotted over. "*Ojiichan*, what were you doing? Did you scare yourself again?"

"Horsey!" the child insisted, raising his plump arms toward the animal, squeezing his sticky hands into fists and releasing them over and over. No doubt recognizing the danger, the horse whinnied, stepped back, and tossed its head. The child's mother scooped the boy up.

"Don't put him on the horse," the old man demanded, standing slowly on painful legs. "He's too fat."

"Oh, he's just a baby," the old man's wife said. She reached over and pinched one of the loathsome baggy cheeks. "And the horse carried them both only yesterday."

Grandpa Tetsu moved around so that the horse was between him and the toddler. "Just don't."

The child kicked and arched his back and his mother plopped him down in the dirt, letting him fiddle with the straw horseshoes.

"And he shouldn't play with those either," Grandpa Tetsu said. And then, realizing he had his daughter's attention, he continued with the lecture he'd been building up to. "Look what you did."

He lifted one of the horse's rear legs showing her the sad state of the hoof. "We're lucky this animal didn't go lame. It's a good thing the sun came out and dried everything up. Hopefully they won't rot." He kicked at the dusty ground.

The old man's wife and daughter exchanged a glance. His wife spoke.

"We should be thankful that they are fine and were given a horse to ride. There have been terrible stories recently of men on the roads—"

"What are you doing there? You!" Grandpa Tetsu interrupted. The toddler had given up the straw horseshoes and was placing small rocks one on top of another. "Only people trying to flee purgatory stack stones. Why is he stacking stones?"

The old man stormed over, grabbed the horseshoes and his fish bag, and returned to his place on the safe side of the horse.

"Oh, why don't you play with him, Dad? He's very, very smart," his daughter said.

"He is," his wife agreed. "And he adores you."

Grandpa Tetsu refused to answer. Instead he turned up the bag and shook the remaining fish bones into his mouth. He chomped down hard and screamed. Pain cracked down his jaw and neck.

The surprised horse kicked up its rear legs, just missing him, and danced sideways blowing air from its nose. The boy sitting under the dancing, blowing creature giggled and clapped his hands. His mother took him into her arms again and petted him as if he were the injured one.

Grandpa Tetsu collapsed to his knees, spitting on the ground. The splintering pain clung inside his skull. With his mouth still open, a line of spit connecting him to the earth, he used one trembling hand to dig through the pile of unchewed bones. When he found what he was looking for, he pushed himself up and held his palm out for his wife and daughter to see.

"Look!" he demanded. "Look what that child put in the bag!" There between his thumb and forefinger, a stone; next to it, three teeth cracked in half and a pool of watery blood.

Pain and Bargain—

After that, Grandpa Tetsu shut himself inside the tearoom and wouldn't come out. For two days he refused visitors and left his meals untouched. His only sustenance was small sips of warm tea he slowly maneuvered down his throat by comic head movements and the sweet tobacco he constantly smoked in his long *kiseru* pipe.

The room reeked of blue smoke and unwashed old man. But despite his wife's nagging, he opened the thick-papered windows only when he needed to relieve himself or when he wanted to observe the horse, listen for any more whinnied advice. It was the horse that had warned him. The only one he trusted now. Mostly Grandpa Tetsu spent the days moaning and mumbling to himself.

The pain fluctuated from the cut of a newly sharpened knife to a dull thrum that caused even his toes to curl and tingle. But it wasn't the pain the old man was worried about. What was more terrifying were the ragged tears in the sliding doors that led to the hallway, and how sometimes through these holes there appeared eyes, eyes with long, wet lashes, eyes that didn't blink.

"Keep him away!" he'd shout, knowing how vulnerable he was. "Just let me die in peace."

Once Grandpa Tetsu flung a vase at the eyes, but it only clattered across the wooden floor of the hall, leaving a larger gash in the paper. That evening a frowning mouth appeared, opening and closing, and gulping for air. It looked hungry and Grandpa Tetsu prayed his dying would come quicker.

On the morning of the third day his wife brought him more tea, tobacco, and news.

"Today I heard some interesting gossip," she began.

The old man groaned. Earlier he'd opened the window and now lay on his side staring at the willow tree, watching the horse nibble the leaves off the thin cascading branches. The beast was suspiciously quiet today.

"I heard there is a visiting craftsman from Yukifuru Mountain, Gingumo Temple. His name is Nakanishi and he used to carve Buddhist statues. He excelled in the One-Thousand Armed Kannon. They say he is practically a legend."

She waited for a response. Grandpa Tetsu scratched at a spider-webbing itch on his thigh instead.

"This past spring he gave up carving Buddhist statues and began a more practical, slightly unconventional, and some say much more lucrative profession—he carves false teeth now."

The old man grunted.

"They say that his teeth are made from only the finest woods and are stronger and more comfortable than even your own teeth."

Grandpa Tetsu huffed and sat up, facing his wife.

"Too expensive," he mumbled.

"Yes," she said, lifting the top of the teapot to check the leaves and then replacing it. "We've been looking for something we might be able to trade for his services."

"There's nothing," he said, readying to lie back down.

"I was thinking about the comb my grandmother gave me, the

142

tortoiseshell one, but when I took it out three of the teeth were broken."

"That child again I bet," the old man said. "Always snooping around, getting into things."

"He's just a baby."

"Maybe," Grandpa Tetsu said, an idea dawning on him. "Every craftsman needs his own apprentice, someone to train from an early age."

"You're much too old to learn a new trade. And you know how bad your eyes are."

"Not me." He looked over his wife's shoulder at the doors that led to the hall. Today there were no eyes or mouth or small clutching hands trying to get in.

"What are you talking about?"

"Two birds, one stone. Perfect payment. You said yourself the child was smart. We barely had enough to feed the two of us when they showed up. He'd have a very good life. Besides, what is a child without a father anyway? He'd be paying me back for the teeth he broke."

"How could you think such a thing?" His wife stood and shook her head down at her husband. "I would never allow that."

"Humph," the old man grumbled, arms across his chest. "Just you wait. I know, I've been told. If we don't get rid of that child something terrible will happen. Something worse than this." He motioned to his swollen mouth.

"Who? Who told you such a thing?"

Grandpa Tetsu didn't answer. Instead he reached for the

teapot at the same moment his wife moved to take the tray away. Their hands touched.

"You're burning up with fever." She pulled her hand away and rubbed it.

"Ridiculous. If anything, I'm cold," Grandpa Tetsu said. "And if I do have a fever he probably gave it to me."

"You're impossible. Why do you have to make everything so difficult?" His wife turned on her heel and left the room, her soft steps beating quickly down the hall. He heard her turn and enter the kitchen, heard the slide and slap of the *fusuma* door shutting behind her.

"Well, then you had better make sure you keep him away from me!" Grandpa Tetsu called. The old man shook his fist twice before turning his attention back to the horse pawing the ground under the willow outside the window.

Wood and Teeth—

Two feet in wooden geta crunched the gravel outside. The pause between each footfall a count longer than any normal man's pace. Long strides, weighted strides. He was tall. Even the heavy material of layered robes found Grandpa Tetsu's ears. Not the roughly hewn, patched cloth of a villager—resonant folds, but a fine weave. A man of wealth. Importance. He was carrying something.

Waiting.

"Nakanishi-sensei has arrived," his wife announced, leading the guest into the six-matted tearoom.

Grandpa Tetsu did not look up. The presence at his back was enormous, unmoving on solid feet, eating up the air around it. There was the click and slide of a tray being set down, a ceramic teapot, two cups, two plates on which he heard the clumsy shift of homemade sweetmeats—one by one the items were removed from a tray and placed on the old, veined wood of the low table. Still the ghost of the stranger leaned in. It tried to whisper in his ear, made the skin on the old man's back crawl. Outside the sun was high; cruel today, it baked even the shadows and trembled the long tendrils of the willow.

Under the willow stood no horse.

"He's been like this." His wife offered an attempted apology. Her embarrassment normally would have angered Grandpa Tetsu. But he didn't care. Not anymore.

He listened as his wife bowed her exit. And then he turned, keeping his head low, his eyes down.

"Thank you for coming," Grandpa Tetsu mumbled as he bowed deeply, his forehead touching the matted floor; a hot river of blood pounded his head, burned the nerves in his crumbling teeth, and darkened his vision. He sat up, blinking away the ink in his eyes. He nearly lost his balance again.

"You are very welcome." Nakanishi gave a slight tilting of his great head.

The stranger's skin was a rubbed angry red, his nose long. He had hair the color of stringy clouds and a slate gray sky. It was long and tied high behind his head, the furrows of a fine-toothed comb were still visible. The same-colored beard fell all the way to the intricately braided cord looped around his waist and tucked into his obi. His eyes were copper.

"I am Nakanishi. They call me the carver-dentist." He set several bags and a large wooden box on the floor. "Please lie down. I'll examine your mouth."

Grandpa Tetsu felt a seeping sense of relief at the stoop of the stranger's shoulders. This suggested humility and diligence at his craft. This was a good man, a good dentist. And yet he was obviously powerful. Surely he'd recognize evil if he saw it. If he saw the carp-faced boy, maybe he could stop whatever plight was bearing down. A warm spot of hope fired in the old man's chest. This stranger dentist would help him, could save him, from his deluded family and the evil carp-faced boy. But how to ask?

Nakanishi used a small mirror to catch the sunlight and direct it into his patient's mouth. Fingers cool on his jaw, moving his head this way and that. Fingers that knew every detail of the Buddha's face, the old man thought.

"You're having much pain?" The carver slipped the mirror back into his sleeve.

"Yes, terrible pain. I haven't eaten. I can barely drink. I'm haunted."

"I've heard a rumor that with my teeth you can eat anything you'd like. Even things you couldn't eat before."

"Fish bones?"

Nakanishi paused, then laughed. "Ah, so that explains it. I was going to ask how you obtained such a fine set of teeth. Except for the unfortunate ones of course."

"Stronger than anyone in town." The old man bit down out of habit and winced from the pain.

"I've seen a lot of teeth, and for your age I think these are clearly the strongest, most healthy ones I've ever set eyes on."

The old man smiled at the acknowledgement of his worth.

Nakanishi withdrew a long white rope from a bag and tied back his sleeves. His movements were certain and quick. He opened the box and began removing bundles wrapped in colorful cloth. Through the thin paper doors came the smell of millet boiled in a bit of rice. At the thought of having new teeth that were stronger than his own, the old man's appetite returned.

"It does smell delicious, doesn't it?" Nakanishi said, reading his thoughts.

"Before I begin, I thought you might be interested in seeing this. It's my latest accomplishment."

He untied the smallest bundle. Wrapped inside two sheets of paper he revealed a pair of wooden false teeth. They were beautiful.

"This set is going to a feudal lord."

The carver held the teeth out, turning them for the old man to see. It was then that he noticed and gasped.

"That's right. The four front teeth are real." The carver-dentist tapped them with his fingernail. "That's what brought me to your small town in the first place. Otsubo."

Otsubo was the crazy man who used to live in a shack behind

the town's only basket weaver.

"When I heard about his accident I came right away."

The accident was the talk all around town. Otsubo used to claim that every evening after his bath a fox visited him. One night he tossed a piece of *abura age* out in the yard and watched as the creature gobbled up the treat and immediately turned into a beautiful woman. The woman then began to entice him with her dancing and other female charms. Otsubo was elated, but every time he tried to approach the creature she would dash off into the forest. This happened for three nights in a row until he ran out of deep-fried tofu and had no means to get any more. On the fourth night, Otsubo hid and waited for the fox to appear. When it did he threw a large basket over the creature, thus capturing it. But after some time, listening to the pitiful cries of the lady inside, he lifted the basket to peek. That's when instead of a white-skinned maiden he was met with a wild blue-faced *oni* who chased him through the town and right off a small cliff.

"Those are his?"

The carver nodded, wrapping the teeth in paper again.

"The only thing more expensive than boxwood teeth are real teeth," the carver said. "I wanted to show you the quality of work I do. Now, lucky for you, it looks like I'll have to pull only three teeth. I'll replace them with something that looks like this."

He removed a couple of small wooden chunks from another pouch.

"Real teeth come at a very high price but this wood is durable and will last a good long time." He handed them over for the old man to examine. "Just look how attractive that grain is."

"Smooth," Grandpa Tetsu said.

"They won't split or splinter. I'll carve them to fit after I get rid of those bad teeth and take some measurements."

Nakanishi removed a glazed earthenware jar and two small cups from one of the bags and placed them on the table next to the tea and snacks.

"I was given this by a saké maker in a small town near Edo." He uncorked the bottle and filled both cups with the cloudy white liquid. "Behind his home there is a waterfall and a river so deep and clear you can see straight to the bottom. The children say if you sit at the water's edge and stare quietly you can watch the *kappa* play on the riverbed." Nakanishi handed him one of the tiny cups.

The old man laughed. "I haven't seen a kappa in ages."

"The pure water is what attracts them. It also makes for the best saké."

Grandpa Tetsu turned up the cup and finished it in one swallow; the cold lacerated his jaw and head. "That is good." The carver refilled his cup and left the top off the jar. "Do help yourself. It's included in the price of the teeth." He drank his own cup down.

The old man poured himself another, feeling a little sad when remembering the cost of his three teeth.

"Yes, she's a good animal," Grandpa Tetsu said. "She almost went lame after my daughter rode in on her. Stupid girl doesn't even know how to change a shoe. How's she doing for you?"

"She's doing well. I left her back where I'm staying. The innkeeper said he'd wash and brush her for me. Tomorrow I'm leaving to call on the feudal lord." He tapped the box where he'd replaced the paper-covered teeth.

"That's good. She deserves the best. I'm sorry I got to know her for only a short time."

"I'll take good care of her."

The old man drank another cup of saké, felt his head take a little dive. He watched as the dentist spread out a clean cloth and removed various metal instruments from the box: long-handled and short-handled scissors, several different sized pliers, tweezers, pointy needle-like tools, curled lengths of wire, and a miniature serrated hand saw.

"You're very lucky, you know," Nakanishi said, sharpening one of the needle-like instruments.

"I am?" The old man reached once more for the saké jug. Maybe he was right, it almost felt like his luck was returning.

"I won't need half of these. Today's procedure is simple."

"Oh, good, no pain."

"What I'll do is remove all the broken pieces first. I can use the surrounding teeth as anchors for your new ones." He lifted the wire. "They're very strong and will secure the new teeth perfectly."

Grandpa Tetsu gloated again at the compliment. "Yep, strongest in the entire town."

"I've never seen such fine teeth. How are you feeling?"

"Good, good." He took another sip of his drink. His face and chest and belly were on fire, and he was just about to sink back onto the mat and let the carver-dentist get started. That's when he heard it, the distinct sound of small unsteady footsteps hurrying down the hall.

"He's here!" the old man said, stiffening.

"Excuse me?"

"The boy, the carp-faced boy. Have you seen him yet? You must have seen him. Or are they hiding him from you, too? You have to help me." There was a rush of panic as the old man remembered what he wanted to tell this man.

"It will be all right." The dentist placed two large hands on Tetsu's shoulders. Something like a wasp's sting ignited in his chest. Spread, numbing. He was guided to the floor. One sweeping hand in red, back and forth in front of his eyes. A blur. His eyes too heavy to keep open.

"Ever since," Grandpa Tetsu said, finding his mouth harder to move. But his hearing remained keen, woosh woosh woosh the robes busied about him. The sweet, clean scent of camphor filled his head. "I poked him when he came too close."

"You poked him?"

"With the hot end of my pipe." The old man wanted to explain better, but he was tired, sleepy. He needed to warn the carver-dentist. "He kept coming around, after me. Fish-faced, evil."

The stranger Nakanishi sat silent, his presence smothering.

"I don't know where she got him." The old man's own voice was too loud in his ears, the words malformed by his softening tongue. "He's the reason her husband sent her home. Found another woman. A woman who had normal babies."

"When you're ready, we can begin." The dentist's voice was very near. Three cool fingers touched his cheek.

"The embarrassment," Grandpa Tetsu said. "You must be careful." He gave in and opened his mouth, let the spin take him. Plummeting.

Teeth and Truth—

The western sun drove hot into the old man's back, waking him. He was on his side, a bundle of cloth pushed up under his head. The sticky feel of recent sweat uncomfortable and clammy on his skin. His slow heartbeat a heavy hammer in his temples, in his mouth.

He remembered.

From down the hall he heard the familiar sounds of his wife and daughter in the kitchen, the rhythmic cleaving of a knife through *daikon*. The gaspy air pumped from the billows into a crackling fire. A giggle and talk he couldn't quite hear. There was the smell of grilling sea bream, the unmistakable sweetened soy sauce aroma of boiling *konbu* seaweed. Earthy root vegetables. His stomach growled. A feast, they were preparing a feast? Maybe for him and his new teeth?

With effort the old man opened his eyes, puffy and crusted and nearly sealed shut. The dentist-carver was gone. His bags and bundles and the box had also vanished. The ceramic jar of saké, though, still stood on the table. A squeeze of his hand told him that he continued to hold the tiny cup, it moved in his grip, and he realized he'd probably broken it at some point during the procedure. A shame. It was an expensive cup.

He tried to sit up but there was only more pain. His chest felt bruised as if someone had been kneeling there for a long time. A whimper sounded in his throat. The puddle of drool in his mouth overflowed. Grandpa Tetsu used his swollen tongue to carefully feel for his new teeth, but found his mouth had been packed entirely with wet cloth. He rolled slightly and spit and gagged and pushed the blood-soaked material onto the floor with his tongue.

For a moment he allowed the viscous liquid to drain onto the cloth under his head. Since he couldn't seem to find the strength to get up, he rolled over onto his back. Some saliva ran down his cheek and filled one ear. His right arm, the one he'd been lying on, had gone completely numb. It was going to hurt like hell in about five minutes.

Grandpa Tetsu's tongue set out again prodding the places where the broken and cracked teeth had been. But there was nothing. For a second he thought maybe the dentist hadn't put them in yet. But his tongue slipped all around the inside of his mouth, over the raw, ragged gums, up and down. And he understood.

There was the unsteady patter of feet hurrying down the hall and Grandpa Tetsu tensed. A small hand found its way through a hole in the paper and slung the door open. The toddler came into the room clapping his hands and bending excitedly at the knees.

The old man's stomach heaved and he turned his head and

threw up what little saké he had left in his stomach and quite a bit of blood that he must have swallowed. With much effort, he brought his left hand up to wipe at his inflamed, toothless mouth with the back of his sleeve. It fell heavily across his chest. He wanted to reprimand the child, to yell at him to get out, but he couldn't find his voice either. This was it, he thought. He'd finally been caught.

The child toddled closer. The old man gripped the broken cup tightly. But something was wrong. He twisted his wrist and opened his hand, craning his neck to look down. He opened his fingers. It wasn't a cup at all. There he saw the upper and lower plate of false teeth the dentist had shown him earlier. The one with the four teeth pried from a dead crazy Otsubo embedded in the wood.

"Horsey," the child called and tottered straight past the old man to the open window. There was the faint rustling of long strands of willow, and then in answer, the neighing of a horse, a bray with a very distinctive deeper voice buried underneath. It was telling him something. The carp-faced child laughed and cooed.

So they didn't sell the horse after all. Why would they sell a creature the child loved so much? Instead they'd paid for the old man's surgery with his own teeth. His own perfect teeth. And they must have made a small fortune. Enough to have a feast, he thought.

A squeal from the child brought his attention back to the room. Grandpa Tetsu closed his eyes tight. He wouldn't cry. He never cried. It sounded as if the carp-faced boy had dropped to the mat and had started crawling, slithering actually, closer and closer to the pained and mostly paralyzed man. All he could do was squeeze the fist on his chest, the one with the teeth in it, over and over, and wish for the boy to leave him alone. His eyes screwed shut, he listened as hard as he could. Hot tears escaped his swollen lids.

There came a neighing, the horse's final rebuke. It seemed to call: I told you so.

The old man heard the pop, pop, pop of a hungry mouth opening and closing, moving closer. And then his right arm suddenly jerked. Again. There was a pulling sensation, a sense of pressure over the tingling that told him the limb was waking up.

Pain.

A smell, yeasty and fetid, enveloped him. Grandpa Tetsu gagged. He tried to scream but only managed a strangled cough. He attempted to roll away from the shooting pain, but something pinned his right elbow to the floor. That's when he opened his eyes and gazed down.

The carp-faced boy sat with his back to him, heavy bottom planted firmly in the crook of the old man's arm. The child stopped what he was doing and turned to look over his shoulder, red-smeared cheeks accentuating his toothy grin.

"Please, no, no, no," Grandpa Tetsu croaked, trying to find the strength to swat with his other hand, to kick or pull away. To scream.

But the child ignored the plea. And instead he smacked his

lips, and held up the old man's hand for him to see. The thumb and forefinger were already stripped of all their skin and meat. The bones—the black bones—had been licked clean.

The horse whinnied. Grandpa Tetsu sobbed. And the carp-faced boy thrust the old man's middle finger into his mouth and began to gnaw.

THE MOTHER OF ALL DEVILS

"Do you think I'm ready? I really think I'm ready." Yoichi was the youngest in the temple at thirteen and not ready at all.

"When one's heart is true, one is always open to the Buddha's teachings." Roshi, the head monk with heavily lidded eyes and a granite-cut frown, touched his chest to reinforce his point.

Another non-answer. Yoichi shivered. It was still three hours before sunrise, freezing. He gently kicked the already packed bundle at his feet. He didn't want to show annoyance, just tapping a clod of dirt off his sandal perhaps. Keeping warm. Last time they had gone on the top-secret mission he'd also been instructed to wake up early and prepare a bag. Only he'd overslept and was told later that he'd been a little bit grouchy.

There was no scolding though. Just Roshi directing him to hand his backpack over to one of the other monks and go sit and empty his mind. How could he empty his mind when he was on his own secret mission?

This time, though, Yoichi had been smart. He'd woken up early—thank you carefully hidden iPhone—and crammed a backpack full of cookies and incense, saké and dolls. Offerings. And a few days ago he'd even located the hand-drawn, ridiculously complicated map, taken a photo, and because he knew there was no way he could smuggle his phone on the trek, memorized the damn thing. So here he was, the map in his head, the backpack at his feet, a plan in his heart. He was ready.

"I think it's time." Roshi toddled over to the other monks. There were six of them, all bald heads and flapping robes. Flashlight beams danced wildly as they filled their own bags, tightened the cords of their woven sandals, and picked through the pile, trying to find a perfect walking stick. Yoichi grabbed his pack and hurried over to join the line.

"*Ohayou gozaimasu*," Roshi addressed the men, still fumbling with their gear.

"Good morning," Yoichi replied along with the others, joining them in a deep bow from the waist. He held his a second longer. Never underestimate humility points.

"Are we all ready?" Roshi asked.

A chorus of affirmative answers rang out. Yoichi not only answered yes, he swung his bag onto his shoulder to show that he was ready. Unfortunately, as he did so something shifted in the backpack and the overly peppy voice of a talking doll cried out: *Hold me in your arms!*

Yoichi squealed and jumped at the sound. The row of bald-headed, dress-wearing men beside him tittered. He even caught the stone-faced Roshi stifling a smile.

Times like these he wished he'd squashed his curiosity about Kishibojin and stayed in school. If he'd wanted to learn so much about paying respect and proper action, he'd never have run away from his grandparents' house in the first place.

But he was fascinated by her, her myth, her legend; her horror story. Kishibojin. Yoichi grew up listening to the same tales as everyone else in the valley town. Maybe it was because he'd been orphaned so young, had such an awful life, but more than anyone he knew he wanted to believe the rumors. He wanted to save her. And up until thirty seconds ago he thought today was that day.

"Yoichi," Roshi said, shuffling over and placing both hands on the boy's shoulders.

Yoichi bowed.

"I think you can join us today."

The boy's heart soared. He was being allowed to go, to live the legend that said on certain secret days the monks of Akumu Temple woke before dawn, strapped offerings to their backs, and made a three-hour trek through the pathless forest deep into the mountains. Upon reaching a hidden house, they'd prostrate themselves, mumble a chorus of sutras, and enter. Some would distribute flowers and light incense, while others would leave gifts of food, tea, and toys on a low table. And then they'd leave.

Only one specially trained monk was allowed to approach the goddess, sitting on the indigo-dyed meditation pillow, her back straight, her eyes closed, her face un-aged. She always wore the same pomegranate-red kimono, an obi of golden brocade cinched tightly around her waist. But they say what would really take your breath away was her hair, falling in a black sheet over her shoulders, down her back to the straw-matted floor, the furrows of a camellia-oiled comb visible. The story went that when no one was around she would spend hours combing her lovely hair.

So after the other monks had left, the chosen one would retrieve the key from the hollow of the stone lantern outside her door—after numerous break-ins and two fires, the head *roshi* had deemed it safer to keep it there than inside the temple itself. The chosen one would enter the house a second time, press his forehead to the floor, and chant soothing prayers of respect and devotion. Slowly he'd approach Kishibojin, and when close enough, one at a time he'd remove her shackles and massage balm into her wrists and ankles and neck.

The goddess never moved. She was content. She was happy. This was her penance, as peaceful as a Buddhist statue she sat, her eyes nearly closed and her breath so long you'd think she wasn't breathing at all. But she was. The air in the room was said to crackle with the aliveness of her, even after all these years, all these hundreds of years.

"Are you sure we're doing the right thing?" Chihiru ran her

hand down the rough bark of an oak as she squatted to catch her breath. She was worried she'd overdone it with the hike. Her doctor had given her strict orders to take it easy, even threatened bed rest if he found out she'd so much as done her own shopping at the local vegetable market. He was definitely going to kill her for this.

"I'm positive," her husband Taka said. He stuffed a printed out map into his fanny pack and zipped it shut. He then clapped his hands and made a "tadah" gesture at the small clearing where, pressed so deep into a tangle of trees that Chihiru hadn't noticed it, stood a one-room, sideways-leaning shack. "There it is!"

"Okay, it might be there. But are you sure this is going to work?" Chihiru asked for the one-hundredth time.

She wasn't much for superstition. She had never in her entire life bought one of the popular *omamori* that promised perfect test scores, entrance into university, marriage, and safe driving. Didn't matter. Even without the popular cloth charms she somehow passed her tests, got into university, married, and had never had so much as a parking ticket.

But this was different, Chihiru thought, standing and getting a good look at the hovel. When your luck was as bad as theirs had been, it was either making the leap to believe in fairy tales or sinking into swampy depression.

"Let's just say, my sources are sound," Taka said, patting the bag on his hip.

"I don't know." Chihiru went over and leaned into her husband's arms. "The place looks pretty unlivable. This could be some deserted equipment shed, a place where the *mikan* farmers used to keep their tools, you know."

"Remember my nephew Masa?" her husband asked. "I guess he's some kind of computer genius now. A couple weeks ago he managed to hack into a monk's iCloud account. I think he was looking for monk porn or something. I don't really want to know. But long story short, he found photos of these old documents, all those old myths about Kishibojin, and this map. He remembered us and what we were going through, so he sent it all along."

"Monk's have iPhones?"

Her husband shrugged. "Twenty-first century."

Chihiru still wasn't convinced and Taka seemed to pick that up from the look on her face.

"Listen, Chi-chan, Masa would never joke about this. He knows how much it means to me, to us." He placed a hand on her stomach.

"Yes, you said that."

It wasn't a matter of whether or not the location was correct. It was a matter of whether or not she would let herself believe the silly superstition: that a reclusive old hag could guarantee safe childbirth.

Chihiru had to admit though, it felt good believing, having hope again. The week before their hike and all the way up the mountain she had been buoyant, excited even. But now that she was here, something like a fast-spreading chill snuck up her spine and warned that maybe this wasn't such a good idea after all. Maybe some things weren't meant to be.

"Just remember, no blabbing to your friends or your mom or anyone in that support group of yours," Taka said. "I'm not kidding."

"Ta-chan, if this works I won't tell a single soul anything for the rest of my life." She held up her little finger and pinky swore with her husband. "Promise."

She meant it. They were desperate. Nineteen years of trying, ten of those involving a host of doctors and nurses, needles and more than a few hospital stays. And just when she'd get pregnant she'd have another miscarriage. So much blood. She was growing afraid of her own body, beginning to hate it. Chihiru was forty-four years old and was exhausted. This truly was their last chance.

"Okay, then, let's do this," Taka said. He cupped his hands, leaned down, and spoke in the direction of her belly. "This baby is going to make it. I have a feeling."

Chihiru imagined the warm light she tried to keep around the fetus at all times glowing a little brighter at its father's voice. She smiled and took her husband's hand.

"Remember to be polite," he repeated as they approached the shack. "Whatever you do, don't piss her off."

"There certainly is a lot of salt," Chihiru noticed, stepping over the three-inch wide line that looked like it encircled the entire house.

"She's a goddess. What did you expect? Have to keep the riffraff out."

Chihiru pointed at her nose and they both giggled like they had when they were first in love back in high school and keeping their relationship a secret from their parents and teachers.

Taka knocked. There was a pause just long enough for all of Chihiru's doubts to rise again.

"Come in." The voice sounded far off and thread thin.

Her husband pushed open the weathered door and they stepped inside. The reek of sweat and urine and something animal-like hit Chihiru in the face and watered her eyes. She almost brought a hand up to cover her nose but stopped. Don't be rude.

"*Shitsurei itashimasu*," she said, politely excusing herself for entering.

"*Douzo, douzo*," came the voice. Chihiru looked around for the far away speaker in such a tiny room.

The only light fell from the open door, but rather than illuminate the space, it only drew attention to the glinting clouds of newly disturbed dust motes choking the air.

Chihiru blinked and let her eyes adjust to the gloom. There was junk everywhere, floor to ceiling: bouquets of wilted flowers, toppled towers of unopened gifts, and rotting bowls of fruit and vegetables. But by far the most disturbing items were the hundreds of roughly played-with dolls, every shape and size imaginable, tossed about the room. Chihiru had heard that when a woman got her wish, she would return to Kishibojin with a doll to give as a gift. So maybe the tales were true.

"Is it what you expected?"

Chihiru yelped at the voice that was now very close and much more animated. Her husband shook her hard by the arm, reprimanding what he surely thought was a rude reaction.

She was there. Right there. What Chihiru had mistaken for a large floppy doll thrown awkwardly against a low table moved. It straightened its posture and slid over and up onto a square cushion. It then coughed lightly and beckoned them closer. They went.

There kneeled a tiny old woman demurely running both hands down her threadbare kimono and trying to tug the tattered cloth over an exposed boney thigh. With the heavy chink of the chains that bound her, one hand rose to tuck a flyaway strand of almost transparent white hair behind her ear. The poor thing was nearly bald. This was no goddess, Chihiru thought. Who could have done such a thing?

"*Hajimemashite*," Chihiru said, bowing.

"Welcome." The old woman's sunken smile revealed blackened gums and a rolling tongue. "I apologize for the mess. I'm not able to get about and clean as much as I'd like."

She lifted one arm and shook the links of metal clamped around her wrist. The manacle slid to reveal a raw, weeping wound. A surge of pity and anger filled Chihiru.

"We're sorry for the intrusion," the younger woman said, wondering if she and Taka could remove the bonds and free the prisoner.

"Not at all. As you may have already guessed, I don't get many visitors." The woman indicated her surroundings, still spooky and cloaked in shadow even though the front door was standing wide open.

"Here, here, you must be tired. Would you like some tea?"

The old woman turned to the table she'd been slumped against seconds earlier. There among the boxes, rusting tins, and bottles sat a teapot and three cups.

Chihiru knelt on the floor across from the old woman and took the offered beverage. Taka, after glancing at the sprinkle of stems and seeds and what might have been moss floating on top of the liquid, politely declined his and remained standing.

"*Itadakimasu.* Thank you," Chihiru said and smiled at the toothless, swaying old woman.

She sipped the bitter, slightly nutty-flavored drink. It warmed her tongue and throat despite being icy cold in her hands and on her lips.

"May I ask why you've come? Are you lost?" The old woman's rheumy and wandering eyes suddenly fixed hard on Chihiru. Her gaze then dropped to take in the bulge of the younger woman's belly.

Her voice turned severe. "Or do you want something?"

"We—," Chihiru didn't know what to say. She finished her tea, letting the contents burn her insides, and set the cup back on the table. Her husband answered for her.

"I know we're not supposed to be here," Taka said. He had unshouldered his backpack, removed several wrapped gifts and was pushing them across the floor. One of the packages hit an antique-looking boxwood comb and sent it sliding, bumping into the thick cushion where the old woman sat.

"There you are," she said, picking it up and examining it in the light. With trembling fingers she plucked a knot of white hair from its teeth, tossed it aside, and tucked the comb into the soiled obi around her waist.

It was then Chihiru looked down. With horror she realized what she'd mistaken for gray, linty dust bunnies were actually balls of hair. Matted into the dirt and filth, covering the wooden floor and sticking to her jeans, endless snarls of long hair.

"We have a problem only you can help us with," Chihiru blurted out. She was hoping to quell her rising terror by engaging the woman directly.

"I thought so." The crone reached over and patted the younger woman's knee.

All at once Chihiru's head began to spin and her joints felt loose and oily. But even more astonishing, against all reason, she suddenly felt protected, like no one could possibly harm her or her baby. It was an inner confidence she hadn't experienced in a very long time. Coming here was the right thing to do.

"You are the mother of all children, guardian of safe childbirth. We came to implore you to help us."

It was as if some long straining binds had been slashed through with a knife. Chihiru started talking and she couldn't stop. She told the decrepit, nodding woman her story, told her thoughts and actions, worries and secrets. Told her things she had never told her husband or her god. When she finished there was a moment of uneasy silence. Chihiru felt exhausted, but also, at the same time, lighter, unburdened.

The older woman instructed her to lie down, a repulsive

thought, but Chihiru did it because this was her very last chance to have a baby of her own, and she knew it.

"Chi-chan, I think it might be time for us to go," her husband's voice was less certain. He was afraid. She ignored him and lay on the disgusting floor.

Chihiru pulled her shirt up as directed, exposing the low swelling of her belly. The ancient woman's twig-like fingers tickled across her skin, before they began kneading. The fingers were delicate and precise, and after some time they seemed to pierce the flesh and reach inside. Chihiru felt them as curious tendrils exploring, before the painful tugs and pressure began. It was the good kind of pain, though, like when your tongue worries a gash in your gums. For the first time she could ever remember, Chihiru felt it was okay to hurt.

"May I ask you something?" the younger woman blurted out, her head still dreamy, afloat.

"Douzo. Go right ahead."

"Is it true? The stories?" Eyes closed, she was no longer on the floor, or even in the room. She was someplace *other*, some scratched-away hollow where mercurial treasures are stored for safekeeping. She wasn't frightened at all.

"What stories?" The old goddess's hands slipped around Chihiru's side to examine her back. As they did so, they dragged the cold links of chain through the grit and hair until they rested heavy upon Chihiru's pregnant belly. She was once more anchored to the floor and the earth beneath it.

"Chi-chan, that's not a polite subject of conversation.

Remember what we talked about?" Taka's voice was jarring. She had forgotten he was there. Chihiru could feel his wariness of the goddess, Kishibojin, and his wanting to rescue her from some threat only he perceived.

"The stories about how you used to be. About how you had hundreds of children and cared so deeply for every single one of them." Chihiru pushed herself up on her elbows.

The crone stopped working and sat back. Chihiru looked deep into her milk-stirred eyes. She hadn't blinked yet, not once since they'd entered the room.

"But your children were starving," Chihiru continued. "You loved them so much, there was nothing else you could do, you had to steal people's babies and feed them to your own. Is it true?"

There was a tight intake of breath from her husband. Chihiru didn't even look over, but from the sound she could tell he'd moved a couple steps closer to the door.

"It's true," the old woman said.

"Chihiru, that's enough. Get up and come here right now." Taka hissed under his breath.

He was making no effort to retrieve her. She continued staring into the mother goddess's kind eyes and stifled a smile. It was all very funny. She could so vividly imagine Taka standing in his annoyed pose, right hand massaging the back of his neck, left one in a fist by his side ever so gently hitting his thigh. Stuck that way. Useless. Always useless.

"Is it true you met the Buddha?" Chihiru continued. She sat all the way up and hugged her knees. "Did he actually take your favorite son and hide him under a rice bowl until you were so distraught with grief that you repented and promised to protect all mothers and children from here on out?"

"Yes, yes." The crone threw her head back, slender neck threatening to snap like a stem, and cackled.

"That's wonderful," Chihiru said. Despite the detached feeling that glazed her head, her middle felt stronger. Taka had been right. This baby was going to make it. "You must have so loved your children to do that."

The old goddess crooked her finger and placed it under the younger woman's chin, lifting it. Chihiru felt a kinship between them. All she wanted was to love a child. She wanted a chance to love her own son or daughter as much as Kishibojin had loved her children. She had that much love in her, and she deserved it.

"Chihiru, you're being rude. We really need to go." Taka was yapping on again. Do this. Do that.

She looked over her shoulder at him. He was at the door now, glancing back and forth between the room and his freedom. Something frightened moved behind his eyes.

"Oh, you're not going to leave, are you? Why don't you stay? I can fix you something." Kishibojin stood, the sound of weighty chains sliding across the floor, the quiet when the woman reached her full height and they were pulled taut. Chihiru looked up, surprised at how tall the goddess really was.

Kishibojin was obviously lonely. No one ever came to visit. Those horrible monks kept her up here, locked away. By the looks of the flowers and the reek of rotten food, they hadn't been in several months at least. It wasn't fair. Chihiru wanted to stay. She needed to help the poor tethered creature.

"I'd love it if you fixed something," Chihiru said, ignoring the pleadings her husband was mewling at the door. "Maybe I can help."

"That you can do," Kishibojin said. Her smile was genuine and made her look years younger. "Are you hungry, dear?"

There was a beat when the air shifted and Chihiru realized the old goddess wasn't talking to her or her husband. Something stirred in the shadowy corner to Chihiru's right. It was then that the sudden realization hit her: They weren't alone in this small shack. Chihiru's throat tightened. Her heart raced. She'd made a horrible mistake.

A stack of wooden boxes clattered to the floor, and another one of those limp over-sized dolls moved. There was a grunt of affirmation, and a smacking of lips. He stood.

"I think it's time to eat," the crone stated, her voice sweet and lilting.

Chihiru sat frozen as Taka moved to make his escape. But he didn't have a chance. The large man—a giant child really—came leaping from the shadows, bolting across the floor with such speed that Taka didn't even have time to move. With one enormous swing he cuffed the terrified man on the side of the head and sent him sprawling.

"No!" Chihiru screamed. She tried to push herself to her feet, but there was no strength in her legs. "M-m-maybe we should be going."

The man-child stood backlit in front of the door frame. Chihiru couldn't make out his expression. All she saw were his meaty shoulders heaving. All she heard was the sickly wheeze of his over-sized lungs straining with every inhale and every exhale. The sound came from everywhere at once and made the room seem to close in around her.

"Oh, you don't want to leave just yet," Kishibojin said. "All good deeds must be repaid, you know. I helped you. Now you need to help me."

Taka lay crumpled on the floor. Chihiru could make out his sobs. He was crying. Despite the situation and the sureness of her death, it struck the younger woman as odd that she'd never seen her husband cry before. All these years and losing so many babies and he'd never cried.

Chihiru turned and looked up at the old hag who had been so kind and saved her baby. She was Kishibojin now, taller with hair thick and blue-black and falling straight to the floor. The skin on her feet, the legs bare behind the torn kimono, her arms, neck, and face smooth and porcelain white. Even the cloudy eyes that were once confused and pitiful had changed and were now fox-hazel and sharp. Kishibojin focused that lancing stare on Chihiru but spoke to her son.

"Get the key," she said and rattled the chains at the boy giant. "And call your sisters. I have a meal to prepare."

The giant boy grunted and exited the door.

Chihiru closed her eyes when she noticed all the other dolls beginning to stir.

It was a little after sunrise when Yoichi pinpointed what was off about the last hour of their hike. He was concentrating on not thinking about how his thighs had turned to rock and his back cramped all the way up to his neck when it hit him, what was wrong.

It was the silence. No birds, no early morning insect chitter, nothing except the rhythmic huff of heavy breathing and the hollow rattle of bells tied to walking sticks. Eight sticks belonging to eight monks. Not one of them said a word.

Five minutes after his discovery, and the sun was high enough for the men to tuck their flashlights into their cloth belts. Fifteen minutes after that, and they broke the tree line and entered a small clearing. Still no forest sounds. Still silence.

That is until Roshi, who was in the lead, let out a howl.

Yoichi slid the tortuous load from his shoulders and scrambled over to where the others stood, encircling the head monk. They had already dropped their own backpacks and were all casting glances at a tiny dilapidated structure that looked to be growing out of an angry wall of trees. This couldn't be the place. It was too small, just a shack. Had they gotten lost? Yoichi thought he had the map memorized, but he realized early on that he had no idea where they were or where they were going.

Roshi regained his composure and began barking orders. This sent the monks scurrying to the cabin where they waited restlessly for him to catch up.

173

"I'm afraid you might have joined us on an unfortunate day," the head monk said, turning to Yoichi. His sleepy eyes looked more tired than usual. "Come. You have an important lesson to learn."

It wasn't until Yoichi reached the others that he realized the front door was standing ajar. While Roshi calmly searched the stone lantern and the ground around it, the other men fidgeted and hissed nervous whispers to one another between clenched teeth. One of them—a round-faced man with wire-rimmed glasses—kept glancing back over his shoulder and into the forest again and again. He was making Yoichi jumpy as well.

"The key is missing," Roshi announced, standing.

He clasped his hands together and recited a sutra Yoichi had never heard before and couldn't understand. It must be very old, he thought. He wondered what it meant.

When Roshi finished, he bowed once deeply from the waist, nodded to the others, and strode into the miserable hut. One by one they slipped inside, Yoichi bringing up the rear.

He was immediately hit with a fetid reek and that high keening sound he always heard when he woke from a nightmare into a too-quiet room. When he knew whatever it was that had been chasing him all night still lingered close by. There was another sound, too.

What was it? Ticking. A clock? No, it was more familiar than that. But faster than he was used to. Yoichi took a deep breath and then identified the mesmerizing click of sandalwood prayer beads being run rapidly through calloused fingers, and the sound of prayers, barely audible over trembling lips.

Yoichi tried to take in the room around him. It was dark and damp and it felt like being inside some monstrous womb. Why was it so hot? It was much too hot for such a late autumn day. He shouldn't be sweating like this.

Another step closer. He was trying to reach Roshi and at the same time figure out what was wrong with his sight. Everything was tunnel visioned. Black and white, but he could see the head monk as he stood, squatted. Stood again. Another monk unmoving by his side. Roshi would tell him what to do, Yoichi thought. He'd explain everything.

He took another labored step forward. Again it was like a dream, the syrupy movement of a dream. Behind him he heard someone retching, while all around him the murmured sutras and clicking beads reached a fevered pitch. Sobbing?

Yoichi made it to Roshi's side and his gaze fell upon the *zabuton* pillow that lay at the older man's feet. It was the one he had read about. It was the one on which Kishibojin was said to sit, day in and day out. The pillow was thick and embroidered and indented from her many years of meditation. Colorless. It was supposed to be indigo. Something else wasn't right. It was empty.

She wasn't here.

Suddenly the monk standing next to Roshi spun and lunged back toward the door. He clipped Yoichi hard on the shoulder almost knocking him over. But Yoichi caught his balance. He wanted to get angry but knew that was the wrong response and defeated the emotion. He smiled and congratulated himself on not losing his temper.

He blinked. And that's when his vision clicked back into color. Red. A whimper escaped his throat. Red, he thought. It was everywhere. Red.

Yoichi looked down and saw the color working its way up the hem of his long robes. It had already soaked his straw sandals, gelling between his toes and itching at the hair on his calves. It almost felt like the sticky, drying mess wanted to hold him there.

Something had died, Yoichi's mind stuttered as he tried to process what had happened in the one-room shack. An icy fist pumped at his heart. Kishibojin?

"Death is not to be feared by one who has lived wisely." Roshi held out a long bone and turned it over in the dim light for Yoichi to examine. It looked like it had been licked clean and there were marks on it. The gnawing teeth marks of an animal?

"Wh-what happened? Did something get in? A bear?" Yoichi asked. It was a ridiculous question and the older monk's ever-present frown vanished for a second and he chuckled.

"You think this is her? No, no, boy. This."

He used the femur to indicate the horror show all around them. "This is someone who was not supposed to be here. An intruder. There were probably two of them. They usually come in pairs."

Yoichi gulped. He couldn't stop the drowning feeling that was overtaking him. He didn't want to know what had happened.

"The goddess then. Where is she?"

Roshi held up his robes and led Yoichi back to the front door.

He pointed at the salt all the monks had been so careful to step over when they crossed the clearing. Now he saw there was an obvious break in it farther down.

"Someone came in and freed her?" Yoichi asked. It should have been him. It had been his plan to let her go. It was why he entered the monastery. He was supposed to free her.

"No," Roshi said calmly, a little sadly. "She's free, yes. But the salt." He pointed with the bone, indicating that whoever had run through the white ring was fleeing the hut, not trying to enter it. "She let one go."

Yoichi was confused. He repeated the statement as a question, "She let one go?"

"I'm sure it was the mother," Roshi continued. "She always lets the mothers go."

"Then this is?"

"The husband," Roshi said, a smug almost giddy half-smile on his face. "A man."

Yoichi felt the sweat turn to ice on his skin.

"Kishibojin is sworn to protect mothers and children. The fathers are never awarded such a courtesy.

"It's one of the reasons this is such a perilous job." Roshi held the bone up in the morning light and used a fingernail to pick away at something on the shaft. He tucked it neatly into his belt beside his flashlight, and slapped his hands together as if to clean them. "She finds all men quite useless."

PINWHEELS AND SPIDER LILIES

The first time the mountain witch appeared, Akito was unprepared. He was scrubbing the moss and lichen off a leaning gravestone. Concentrating so intently, he didn't notice that the prickly *tawashi* clenched in his hand was piercing his skin. That is, he didn't notice until he emptied a bucket over the newly scoured slab and saw the water run red.

Akito forced himself to smile. The pain was almost enough to piss him off again. But not today. He dropped the scrub brush and filled his lungs with autumn air. Sweet olive trees. Acorns. The candy-like smell of birch and discarded talismans smoldering in the temple's burn barrel.

Akito's mantra for the past eighteen hours had been "Get rid of the rage and everything will be all right again." He finally understood it. There was nothing to get upset about in life. A man had to be thankful for what came his way. This was a completely new concept to Akito thanks to the epiphany he'd had just that morning.

"What do you have to give me?" The voice came, whispered behind his left ear. Akito jumped, twisting and banging his knee on the stone.

"*Chikusho!*" he cursed and kicked the grave twice with his heel. There was no one behind him.

A tittering laugh—a sound that felt like a nest of insects had been loosed inside his shirt—brought his attention to the crooked oak in the opposite direction of the voice. There, a woman dressed in the layered silks of an *oiran* reclined unnaturally against the tree. How had he not seen her? How long had she been watching him?

With a hand dripping fingernails so long they curled, she brought a metal *kiseru* pipe to the thin cut of her mouth and inhaled. Her eyes rolled back in her head and she moaned in a way that made Akito uncomfortable.

He thought it proper to look away but before he could, his attention fell to her skeletal knee protruding from the filthy and torn fabric of her kimono, and then to her other awful hand, those abnormal nails picking absentmindedly at the scabs and boils covering it. His stomach turned.

When the crone exhaled, blue smoke clouded the air and a spicy, peppery reek pinched Akito's throat until it narrowed like a reed. For a second he thought it might close entirely. Panic fluttered in his chest. The witch laughed again and his throat opened.

"What do you have to give me?" she repeated, slower this time.

"I-uh, I…"

Akito had nothing. Yesterday morning his boss had called him into his office and fired him from his job of fifteen years. That evening his adoring, ungrateful bitch of a wife kneeled down in front of the TV and demanded he leave the house. "Right this minute," she'd said. She'd had enough. The words she used were almost exactly the same as the ones his boss had shouted hours earlier. His life was shit, but at least now, given his new point of view, he had to chuckle at the irony.

So in typical Akito fashion, after obeying his boss, last night, a little after ten, he bowed his head and obeyed his wife. He heaved himself off the sofa and left the house. With no idea what to do or where to go, he wandered the streets for hours, dragging his tired ass farther and farther away from the city, growing angrier and angrier as he did.

It must have been around midnight, freezing, starving, and feet-wrecked—he was not sure he could take another step—when he caught the scent of wood smoke on the wind. He looked up, and there leaning into one another stood the yellowing, cobwebbed lights marking the front gate of the old cemetery. Just beyond them, the rusting barrel the monks kept filled and burning at all times was beckoning him with its heat and dancing orange blaze.

Akito slept more soundly than he had in years, curled up on the dead grass next to the warm furnace of the popping barrel. He dreamed he saw the outlines of tiny people in every licking flame, all of them animated, tearing at their clothes and skin. Their howling lulled him to sleep. Peaceful.

Peaceful, that was, until morning when the butt end of a rake jabbing at his ribs woke him. A monk from the temple, come to tend the fire.

It was at that moment—blinking up at the bald man in the black robes silhouetted against predawn blue—Akito had the epiphany. It's all a matter of perspective, he thought. A man could be below another in status, financial gain, love, but still be very comfortable. Happy even.

For the first time he finally saw life and his part in it, saw it for what it really was. Akito was a man whose luck always ran from shitty to mediocre and back again. Like the time he won the lottery. Yeah, he won the lottery, but only five thousand yen. It was only enough to buy himself a *shabu-shabu* dinner and a bottle of Isojiman *nihonshu*, not enough to make a dent on his mortgage or pay off his car loan.

His luck was a cycle he couldn't break, and it would always be that way. What Akito realized he had to do was be grateful for whatever he got. Because it was enough.

Sure, yesterday was without a doubt his worst day, but today he woke up, had a revelation, and discovered his fortune had taken its usual modest upturn. The old Akito would curse the fact that he no longer had a salary or a family, but today's Akito was thankful for the new gig: a groundskeeper at the cemetery.

All he had to do was scour, weed, and tidy the hundreds of stones sunk into the foot of Mount Jigoku and halfway up its side. There was no pay, but he was given permission to any of the offerings left in front of the headstones by attentive friends and family—candies, rice crackers, booze.

There was one catch. They could only be consumed after they'd sat out for at least forty-eight hours. Two days, Akito was told by the monk with the rake, was the proper amount of time to wait for the gods to absorb all of the godly nutrients necessary to sustain them in their heavenly duties.

He was assured that except for the occasional soggy box of Pocky—due to the elements and not the gods' appetites—there would be no difference in taste. Not only the new job, but also he was given a futon and allowed to live in the toolshed for as long as he needed.

Food. Shelter. Working in the great outdoors. He wouldn't starve. He wasn't homeless. And he was getting exercise without an expensive gym membership. Who needed a pension anyway?

The witch took another inhumanly long drag on the poisonous pipe. Something in her throat rattled, sounded almost like a growl.

Akito frantically patted the pockets of his pants. Empty. The monk had been kind enough to give him some work clothes to wear; much better than the pajamas he'd left the house in last night. Warmer, too.

What did he stash in the toolshed when he changed? What did he grab from the kitchen table when he was so callously thrown out on the street? His wallet. But there was hardly any money in it. His wife had cut up his credit card two months ago. Did a mountain witch even have use for money?

"I've lost everything." Akito stopped his futile search and addressed the impatient witch again.

"Oh, I don't think that's true," she said. "How about a trade? You give me something? I give you something in return?"

Akito was very aware that these weren't questions. He looked down and saw the bloody handprints he just slapped all over the pockets on the right side of his new beige trousers. He remembered the pain in his cut palm. It was so like him to ruin the gift of a nice pair of pants. He felt the coil of self-hate stir in his gut again. Get rid of the rage. It'll be all right, he told himself.

"I might have..." Akito's courage faltered.

The witch was gazing in the opposite direction, into the dark, perfectly quiet forest. Now was his chance. He slowly retrieved the bottle he'd been nursing all day from its place in front of the grave and took three long gulps. The liquid seared his throat again as it went down. Had he yelled? He couldn't remember.

"I think I might have something in the toolshed. I'll go check," he said. "I'll, um, be right back."

The witch turned to scrutinize him once more and chuckled her uncanny laugh, a laugh that slithered alive under all the lengthening shadows. It unnerved him. An icy wind sent the pinwheels that decorated every gravestone clicking and spinning. Red, blue, yellow, some glossy and new, others worn and faded, they ticked and spun in unison. Akito had the unsettling feeling he didn't have much time.

He trotted off, surprised at how deeply sore his muscles were, down-to-the-bone tired. He really was out of shape. He didn't think he'd been working that hard. He hadn't even moved to a new stone yet, still working to get that first one clean. He had to admit the all-over aching was a better feeling than the cramping back and stiff shoulders that came with sitting at his desk all day.

Akito considered the color of the sky. Only a couple more hours of light. After he got rid of the witch, he'd wear himself out, finish the bottle, and collapse on his moldy-smelling futon. He'd then pray to the heartless gods that he wouldn't dream.

Akito burst into the equipment shed, out of breath and screaming.

"Fuck the suit and tie! Fuck the bus, the two trains, and the twenty-minute zombie walk to the fourteenth floor of an office building to hunch in front of a computer in a room full of fifty other idiots all hunching in front of theirs."

He stomped over to the bench where he'd left all his worldly belongings. One wallet. One set of keys. One cell phone, the battery long dead. One crumpled handkerchief still damp from last night's tears.

"Fuck the morning exercises and the *chorei* meetings, the unpaid overtime and the USB stick I might have lost on the train, the one that was supposed to be oh-so-important. But that information never came out anyway, did it?" Akito continued his tirade, picking up each item and then slapping it down, deeming it useless. "Fuck a boss who has no heart and a paycheck that is never enough."

He opened his wallet and there in the window where his train pass was supposed to be—he'd lost that a couple months ago—was a photo of his daughter Mai. He'd taken it in August at their neighborhood temple's Obon festival. She stood wearing her yellow *yukata* and holding up a plastic bag full of fish she'd caught in a goldfish scooping game.

He remembered thinking it was the best photo he'd ever taken, the way the red lanterns in the background seemed to lead the eye to her beaming face. The yellow of her outfit and the orange of the fish. He remembered how difficult it was for him to get the picture off his phone and print it exactly the right size so it fit inside his wallet. He had the sudden realization—that must have been when he'd lost the train pass. Maybe he'd thrown it away with the cut off edges of the printer paper. He had been using it for a size reference. Yeah, that's what happened. It was just like him.

He was knocked from his new self-punishment when another thought took its place. Like a stab in his heart he remembered he hadn't been allowed to see Mai before his wife told him to leave the house. She was sleeping and Natsuko wouldn't let him wake her to say goodbye. This time Akito's anger latched on.

He returned to find the crone still waiting. Her thorny

presence planted like a stone in the earth. He needed to shake his bad mood. It wasn't a good idea to provoke her. He took three more gulps of the booze, relished the way it razored his throat all the way down.

Maybe the liquid hurt because the gods were angry. It was true. He hadn't waited the allotted time to pilfer the drink. In fact, he watched the bereaved family toddle down the hill and get into their car, snatching the gift they'd left before they'd even gotten their seatbelts fastened.

He stoppered the bottle and set it back down. No, the gods didn't know what he'd done. The gods weren't heartless. The gods didn't exist at all.

"So what do you have for me?"

The mountain witch pushed herself up from her reclining position to better face him. She tucked her chin and cocked her birdlike head, her neck so thin that it nodded under the weight of her disheveled hair, oiled and twisted, secured with twine and combs. Long pieces spilled over her shoulders and writhed across the ground. Tiny bells hung from long metal pins decorating the dreadful tresses. When she stood, the bells chirred like crickets, hypnotizing. She was huge. Akito couldn't take his eyes off the monster as she approached.

"I really have lost everything," he said.

His body hummed from exhaustion. The sun had already sunk behind Mount Jigoku, and the cooling air was chilly on his skin. It would be dark very soon.

"I lost my job. My wife kicked me out of my house—" before

he could finish his plea, a sappy branch exploded in the burn barrel sending up a shower of sparks.

It sounded like a warning. He knew he was giving excuses and that wasn't a good idea, given his audience.

The mountain witch took a step forward. Akito's legs went momentarily weak at her approach. Nightingale dung ran bleached lines down her cheeks and down her slim neck. She stopped once to adjust her pitiful robes as if she had all the time in the world. When she was satisfied, she sauntered over.

"I'll take any old thing," she said, circling him. She smelled of camellias and ash and something long dead. "This is a trade, remember?"

She pressed against him, the heat of her, the reek of her smoky, putrid breath, the sweet oil caking her hair and staining the collar of her kimono.

"Tell me what you want first, then we can talk about the deal," the witch said.

Was he really being given a second chance? Could he get his job back, his family back, his life back? Was his luck finally improving?

Akito didn't fit in. He never had. His coworkers never invited him out for drinks. His wife didn't understand the stress of work. He always tried too hard and ended up making ridiculous mistakes. He said the wrong things. Ever since he was a child he always blundered. If it were true what this old hag was saying, if he could get it all back, he'd do it right this time. This time he wouldn't fuck up.

"My little girl," Akito blurted out. "Her name is Mai. She's six. My wife, Natsuko, has been turning her against me. The last thing she said before she slammed the door on me was that I would never see her again. Mai."

"I understand." The witch tucked her kiseru pipe into the thick obi around her waist. She dragged one long, cracked fingernail down his cheek, lifted his chin. "Your daughter, Mai."

Akito nodded.

"What do you have to give me?"

He didn't think it would be enough, but he had to try. He plunged his blood-sticky hand into his pocket and handed her his keys.

Two

The second time the mountain witch appeared, Akito was ready. At least he thought he was. He spent the morning combing the cemetery, sifting through the offerings, a tin of cookies, a handful of marbles, a bowl of persimmons. Then there were the dozens upon dozens of stuffed animals, all in varying degrees of wear and tear. Around all of their necks were tied bibs, some store bought, some handmade, many stitched with the names of children who would never get to wear them.

Akito was squatting with his back to the mountain, lining up the presents, when he had the sensation he was no longer alone.

An involuntary shudder rattled him, and he turned to look

into the forest. He expected to see the mountain witch looming in the tree line, but she wasn't there. The dense tangle of trees was somehow blacker and more silent than he remembered it being yesterday. He glanced up to check the crooked branches of nearby trees, searched the moss-covered granite stones. There was no one. But he couldn't shake the feeling he was being watched, that some presence was very close. Akito snatched a warm can of beer from the items he'd stolen, opened it, and drank until his hands stopped shaking.

Movement down at the foot of the cemetery caught his eye. Someone was here. He hadn't heard the sound of gravel popping under tires as it did whenever a car entered the parking area. He jumped to his feet.

There he saw her, a little girl, bouncing through the front gate. She seemed to be at ease with her surroundings, not afraid or confused as she zigzagged through the stepped maze of gravestones, collecting the ticking pinwheels and snapping off the crisp stems of blood-red spider lilies as she made her way in his direction.

Akito felt an enormous weight fill him, a weight that instantly ballooned and lightened him. He called out.

"Mai!"

The little girl looked up and waved. She was wearing the Tonari no Totoro pajamas he'd bought her for her birthday, the ones that had Totoro standing at a bus stop holding an umbrella over his head, eyes startled wide. He saw his daughter's mouth move as she yelled something into the wind, but he couldn't hear.

She quickened her pace.

"Mai, my baby. Mai-chan." He finished his drink and was about to hurry and meet her when the voice stopped him.

"What do you have to give me?"

Akito's heart seized. He turned to face the mountain witch, hovering, surrounded by undulating veils and curls of blue-gray smoke and hair so long that it pooled on the ground.

"*Arigatou*," he said, bowing deeply. "Thank you. You got her away from her mother. You brought her to me."

"But what do you have to give me today?" The heavy-lidded eyes stared down at him.

Akito motioned to the carefully laid out offerings at his feet. The witch grunted and spat on a stuffed bear.

"*Gomi*," she said. "Garbage."

"But—"

"What do you have to give me today?"

Akito's mind raced. His hands went again to his empty pockets. He watched helplessly as his little girl skipped closer and closer. If he didn't pay up with something new, would the crone whisk her away? Take her back to her mother? A rise of panic tightened his chest.

He watched as his daughter reached the top row of the cemetery, the row where he stood with the towering hag. Mai had stopped at the opposite end and was arranging her plucked flowers and pinwheels in her arms before she looked up at him again.

"Papa!"

"Mai-chan!" Akito knelt and held out his arms. He hadn't showered in two days and cringed at the stench emanating from his body. He hoped Mai wouldn't notice.

"I'm still waiting," the old crone said from behind him. "Another trade."

He thought he felt her sharp-clawed hands slip around his neck and jumped. He looked back, but she was still standing, gnawing on the metal end of the pipe, peering down at him with mischievous, drowsy eyes.

"Let me think," he said. "I'm sure I have something."

How long could he stall?

The buoyancy returned when he saw Mai hurtling toward him. The little girl squealed as she ran, hair trailing behind her, a giant pinwheel and spider-lily bouquet hugged tightly to her chest.

"Papa," she cried and fell into his arms. He held her, breathed deep her shampoo-scented hair, something floral his wife always used, the clean milky smell of the skin on her neck.

Mai pushed herself away giggling. She looked down at the gift she'd made.

"Half are for you and half are for Mama." She plopped down on the dirty ground and began dividing up the long-stemmed presents equally. She was a kind child. She'd always been a kind child. It was then that he knew what he had to do.

Akito turned and met the mountain witch's eye, a smirk hitched up half her face. She cocked her head as if reading his mind.

"We used to be happy," he said. "A family. It was work that

did it. That tore us apart. But there was a time, I can remember it now, when we were a family."

Akito was overwhelmed with emotion, remembering when his wife was a different woman. Had he been a different man, too?

"I still love her," his voice clenching his throat.

The crone held out her hand. There was no thought at all. Akito twisted off his wedding ring and dropped it into her palm.

Three

The third time the mountain witch appeared it was the last time, the last test. Akito didn't know that though.

It was late afternoon and he was returning from his hike into town, an hour there, an hour back. Or was it more? Less? He didn't have a watch, and he'd thrown his useless brick of a cell phone in the barrel of flames back at the cemetery. Time had become nebulous and inconsequential. Even the sun didn't quite move across the sky at the right speed.

It didn't matter, though, what time it was. All Akito knew was that he was in a hurry to get back. His nice work clothes were soiled, his feet were blistered, and he reeked. But that didn't matter either. He couldn't keep the bounce from his step or the smile off his face. He didn't dare say it out loud because he might jinx it, but for the first time in years he was truly happy.

He had woken that morning on the floor of the toolshed with Mai sleeping next to him. Her two tiny fists were balled up under her chin, holding a threadbare blanket to keep off the chill. Hoping it would help, Akito tucked the ends of the cover around her, but the movement made her thrash and cry out in her sleep. He imagined the tiny little girl was trying to escape her dreams. Nightmares?

Akito brushed the hair from her forehead and whispered over and over.

"It's okay. It'll be okay."

The little girl calmed down and opened her eyes. When she saw her father she smiled and implored him again.

"Tell me about the day I was born."

Akito told her once more the story about when he was driving her mother to her grandmother's house. It was tradition that a pregnant mommy go to her own mommy's home to have her child. There she would be taken care of properly and also learn how to care for the new baby properly. He explained that they were halfway to grandma's house when her mother went into labor. Mai wanted to be born right then and there. His daughter squealed by his side. She did every time he got to that point in the story, no doubt excited about the control she had over her own life, even at such a young age.

Akito went on, embellishing the parts where strangers pulled over to help and how one of those strangers just happened to be a man who was a paramedic on his way home from work. The luck.

The story ended the same as it did the half dozen other times he'd told it, with great flourish about how Mai had been born right there on a Tomei highway exit ramp and how after the off-duty paramedic announced she was healthy, the gathered crowd cheered and one elderly man cried out "banzai" three times, throwing his arms into the air with each shout.

"We almost named you Michiko, Street Child," he said and Mai laughed and laughed. Akito's heart was full.

Yesterday, after the mountain witch had vanished with his ring, he worried his little girl might be upset at having been taken from her mother. Even more, he worried she'd whine and throw a tantrum and the monks would come down from the temple and chastise him; or worse, some random mourner might call the police and his luck would plummet back to his default level of pure shit. Could he go to jail? He didn't kidnap her himself. But as the day progressed he realized his worry was a waste of energy.

She might be an ugly old hag, but Akito trusted the mountain witch's promises. He'd convinced Mai that her mother was coming to join them soon and that they'd be a family again. Then, to further pacify the little girl, he'd told her the funny and exciting story of when she was born. The story not only soothed Mai, but it also reinforced his conviction that he was a changed man. He did remember those old feelings. He did still have them. He was confident he could save this marriage, this family.

He didn't know why, but the scene played out vividly inside his head. Natsuko would arrive much like Mai had, magically set down by the cemetery's front gate, not sure how she got there or why. But then she'd look up dreamily and see, there among the gravestones, her husband and daughter.

194

Mai would be sitting on one of the marble plinths, swinging her feet and playing with the toys he had collected. Beside her, he'd be working hard, scrubbing or raking or weeding. He had to get past this first gravestone before he moved on to the next. His wife would notice that while he'd only been gone three days, he'd lost some weight and gotten a little bit of a tan. He looked stronger, even handsome maybe. She'd then note that father and daughter were talking animatedly and laughing, and while she wouldn't be able to hear the conversation, her heart would soften at the sight and she'd realize her mistake.

His wife of ten years would regret all those years of coldness and bitterness, heartlessness. Like Akito, she'd suddenly recall how it used to be between them. She'd remember her past feelings, too.

It's all a matter of perspective, Akito thought. It wasn't just him who could change. Natsuko could change, as well. He was sure of it.

When he reached the gates of the cemetery, he was relieved to see that his wife still hadn't arrived. Soon. Before dark, she'd be here. But the sun had already dropped behind the mountain, and the sky was lit up in brilliant streaks of pink and orange. Night insects buzzed in the grass, but as he'd grown used to, the forest beyond was still. There wasn't any breeze. It was colder than yesterday. Winter felt very close.

Akito trudged up the side of the hill, picking his way through the graves, groceries swinging in his uncut hand. He was wishing he'd bought a blanket for Mai. But he only had enough money for the cold milk, Pocky, and two tuna rice balls.

"Mai-chan!" he hollered, suddenly anxious about leaving her all by herself for so long.

It was a good idea at the time. He'd left her having a tea party with all the stuffed animals. Soggy dogs missing eyes, dolls so old they'd gone bald, their plastic faces half melted and baked dark brown from years in the sun. His daughter was a sweet-tempered girl and treated them all equally, no matter how hideous or malformed. Akito wondered what she would be when she became an adult. A nurse maybe.

"Mai-chan!" he yelled again.

The little girl popped her head up between two graves and waved down at him. She held a finger up to her lips and then disappeared once more. He imagined she must have put the stuffed animals down for the night. They were all sleeping and she didn't want his calling out to disturb them. Such a sweet little girl. He prided himself on his tactic for leaving her alone.

Before he left, Akito had spread out a blue tarp he'd found in the equipment shed for her to play on. He'd heaped all the dolls, stuffed animals, and edible-looking snacks he could pilfer from the graves in the middle.

"Whatever you do, don't step a foot off the blue square. You're safe here. You're invisible," he warned. "You see up there?" He pointed to the wall of trees.

"There are evil witches who live in that forest and if they see little girls playing off the tarp, they'll swoop down and grab them and take them home to feed to their own children."

It worked. Something bad could have happened in those two-and-a-half hours he was away, but it didn't. Mai hadn't even strayed. Good girl.

It wasn't until Akito crested the last row of gravestones that he saw what was keeping his daughter's attention. His heart took flight again. His fantasy had been wrong. She was there. Natsuko, his wife, lay curled up in the middle of a blue sea. She was surrounded by a circle of dilapidated stuffed animals and dolls. Mai sat next to her, holding up the same finger to her lips. When she saw that her father understood he was to be quiet, the little girl lay down next to her mother and scooched herself into the sleeping woman's arms.

Akito trotted the rest of the way, slowing only when he got close. He set the shopping bag down and tiptoed over. He didn't want to wake his wife. He wanted to surprise her, show her how much he'd changed. It would take some adjusting, he knew. But it had worked out with Mai. It would work out with Natsuko, too.

Akito stepped onto the tarp and kneeled down next to his wife and daughter. They were beautiful. He was patient. At least he was now. He'd let them sleep.

What had changed? Was it simply that he was finally genuinely thankful for what he had in life, however meager it was? A shitty little job and a shitty little hut to live in. Maybe it was because, for the first time, he didn't want anything at all, and the uncaring universe and callous gods noticed and decided to reward him with all this.

There was a sudden shriek from the forest. Goose bumps

spider-walked up his spine and neck. Natsuko and Mai didn't stir. Akito stared into the forest. Today it threatened again, blacker, more terrible.

The mountain witch was coming. He could tell by the electric way the air shivered on his skin and the hush that settled in the cemetery. The crickets in the tall grass had stopped their chirping. No twigs broke. No leaves rattled. The only sound when she approached was the crackle of flame from the burn barrel and the occasional pop of sappy wood exploding. She was coming. Her presence was huge.

Akito kept his eye trained on the tree line, and this time he saw her as she stepped from the utter black that painted the space between the trees. He watched her insect legs stretch and find ground, tense and pull her awful body forward. Closer and closer, moving nightmare-like in a shroud of smoke. The smoke became mist and poured down the hill and into the graveyard, covering the ground with a hiss. Akito's breaths were coming in short bursts now. The hag moved too slow and too fast at once. He glanced down to check his wife and child, and when he looked up again the witch was standing right there in front of him.

He wished she wouldn't speak, that gravelly voice would surely wake them. He wanted them both to rest. He knew how magical it felt to sleep on the ground here and he wanted to share that. If the crone just wouldn't speak this time.

But she did.

"What do you have to give me today?" The mountain witch crouched and rested a hand on Mai's small slumbering head. She considered the child, her cheeks hollowing as she sucked on the pipe in the corner of her mouth.

Akito cringed. What would his wife and daughter do if they woke and saw her there? They'd be terrified. Would they blame him? Or maybe he could comfort them, tell them it was okay, the witch was a friend of his. She was helping him.

"I don't need any more," Akito said. He knew he risked angering her, but it was true. There was nothing else he needed. This was it, right here in front of him. There was no more need to be selfish.

The mountain witch's lips curled into that smile that was anything but happy. She opened her mouth to reveal blackened teeth and a leech-like tongue. She leaned down and exhaled gauzy smoke over the mother and child, the nauseating spice of it turning Akito's stomach, spinning his head.

"You don't need any more?" she repeated turning his statement into a question.

Akito looked down. The smoke from the witch's mouth swept away the mist until only the square of blue tarp and what was on it was visible. Akito saw. He remembered.

He'd left work, furious. He loathed his boss, everyone he worked with. They teased him. Bullied him. It was like this his whole life. He couldn't do anything right. He was embarrassed, ashamed. He didn't know what to tell Natsuko about getting fired. It wasn't something they did at his company. No one ever got fired. But he was that much of a loser. Always had been. He and his wife hadn't been getting along. He felt weak around her.

199

Not like a man at all. There was no way she'd understand.

Akito called and told her he was going to work overtime. He went straight to the *izakaya* on the way home. It was eight when he decided he had gained enough courage to talk to her, the woman who was supposed to understand. He made a single stop at the 7-11 for a little more booze and some Pocky for Mai. It was her favorite snack. She liked to stir the cookie end in her milk.

Akito didn't realize how much shittier his luck could get. Once home his keys didn't work in the door. They kept slipping out of his hands. He'd pick them up and they'd fall again. The plastic handles of the shopping bag cut into his palm. Everything was pissing him off. So he banged on the door with his fist. He'd forgotten eight was Mai's bedtime. He wondered why Natsuko wasn't opening the door. He banged harder until she answered.

They had met in university, dated for a year, and then got married. They'd both come from outside of the prefecture and didn't have many friends. Maybe it had been good at first, before they really knew each other. Before she knew him and what a fuckup he was. Before his shitty to mediocre and back again luck drained her of all her ambition and happiness.

She wasn't compassionate when she heard the news about him getting fired. She rolled her eyes. Laughed even. Like they all laughed when he was carrying the cardboard box loaded with everything from his desk, shuffling to the door. He tripped, fell, and went splaying out across the carpet. The box upended and not a single person helped him pick up the mess.

Natsuko's laugh. It was the same laugh.

Something enormous and numbing and black crested inside Akito, a wave too big to hold back. No one could have held it back. He snapped. He reached into the bag and grabbed the bottle he'd just purchased by the neck. It was the largest bottle of *shochu*—sweet potato liquor—they sold. The cheap stuff. The cheapest stuff. The stuff he usually kept hidden in his closet, in the trunk of his car. The stuff that warmed his belly, made soft his troubles. The stuff that fixed everything. At least at first. It was what made him strong in a world where he was very, very weak.

"I loved them," he said to the witch. He couldn't stop looking at the two precious things that slept in front of him.

He reached out and touched Mai's tiny hand, a fist holding Natsuko's finger. She lay so perfectly curled up against the body of her mother, it looked like they were made to be that way.

He remembered again. A flash of a nightmare. A memory. Mai screaming, throwing a tantrum. She'd been woken. His wife telling him to get out, leave, she couldn't take it anymore. Natsuko had pulled her daughter close and turned her back to Akito when he lunged. She'd tried to shield Mai from his rage. She should have run, but she didn't. Why didn't she run? She just huddled there and took it.

Didn't they know how tired he was? Didn't everyone know? How at the end of every fucking day he came home utterly exhausted? Didn't they realize how his entire life he had been kowtowing to someone, a high school bully, the team at the office, his boss, his own father? How he had to bury his pride all the time? And why did they have to piss him off so much? Why did his wife have to nag? Why did Mai have to cry and push him away?

"I'm so sorry," his voice cracked.

His two precious things lay still, not breathing, on a sheet of blue the color of a summer sky. Clothes soaked in red, hair tangled. He could hardly recognize Natsuko, a crumpled messy heap. But Mai. He reached down and touched her exposed calf. With the tips of his fingers he traced his own handprint, so perfectly bruised on her soft skin. He had grabbed her as she tried to scramble away. He had stopped her howling, stopped her escape. His precious Mai. He pulled the cuff of her pant leg down. She was wearing the pajamas he'd gotten her, the ones she loved so much, Totoro standing under an umbrella in the rain. Mai, unmoving, her eyes startled wide.

"I'm so, so sorry," he repeated, and he meant it this time. He really meant it. This time there were real tears filling his eyes. Akito pleaded to all those gods he didn't believe in that he could change this thing he did.

The mountain witch sucked on the metal tip of the kiseru and inflated her chest. The bowl crackled and glowed orange-red. She stood. She was even larger than before. She straightened herself until she reached her full height. The wispy dreamlike quality of her vanished and was replaced with a weight, a realness of her presence that terrified Akito. This wasn't a dream anymore.

"If there is nothing left to give," she said.

The crone reached down and sank one of her taloned hands into his elbow and yanked him to his feet. Akito screamed out in pain.

He wanted to pull away, flee, but her hand pinched harder, nails pierced his skin, enflaming nerves all up and down his arm. He should be angry, Akito thought. But he wasn't. There was no more anger. The very unfamiliar feeling of satisfaction filled his chest. He'd done it. He'd gotten rid of the rage. Everything was going to be all right.

"Let's go for a walk," the crone said, steering him by the elbow. She used the peppery-smelling kiseru to point at the wall of the too-black forest rising in front of them. He hadn't realized how tall it was. The canopy growled as it crawled across the heavens, curving up and over. With every step they took, it devoured more and more light. There was something else, too. For the first time he thought he heard sounds coming from it, distant wailings, moans. A hundred, no a thousand burn barrels filled with screaming souls.

And whimpering. But that was his own.

"Where are we going?" he asked. But he knew.

The mountain witch threw her head back and cackled, sending long snakes of that bluish smoke writhing in the still autumn air. Akito's throat seized up like someone had grabbed it with two fists. He fell to his knees choking, and trying to suck in air. He clawed at his neck with his free hand.

"It's not going to be that easy," the witch said, jerking him back to his feet. She looked down at him and blew the smoke away from his face with her rancid breath. His throat opened again and he gulped like a fish out of water.

"No," she said. "It's not going to be easy at all."

ABOUT THE AUTHOR

Thersa Matsuura is an American expat who has lived half her life in a small fishing town in Japan. Her fluency in Japanese allows her to do research into parts of the culture—legends, folktales, and superstitions—that are little known to western audiences. A lot of what she digs up informs her stories, while the rest finds its way onto her blog (thersamatsuura.com) and into her podcast, *Uncanny Japan* (uncannyjapan.com).

Thersa Matsuura is a graduate of Clarion West (2015), recipient of HWA's Mary Wollstonecraft Shelley Scholarship (2015), and the author of another collection, *A Robe of Feathers and Other Stories* (Counterpoint LLC, 2009). She's also had stories published in various magazines and anthologies including: *Black Static*, *Fortean Times*, *Madhouse* (anthology), and *The Beauty of Death* (anthology)

ACKNOWLEDGEMENTS

First, I'd like to throw the biggest of thank yous to Alessandro Manzetti and Independent Legions Publishing for accepting my short story, "The Carp-Faced Boy," into The Beauty of Death anthology and then reaching out to me afterward to inquire about more stories. Without Alessandro's fondness for an ugly, drooling, truly freaky toddler, this collection would never exist. Thank you to my editor Jodi Renée Lester for taking on that story first, then the collection, and also for informing me the carp-faced boy might have some distant relatives existing in America, too. Thank you Daniele Serra for the beautiful cover art. I've always admired your work and am tickled pink with what you've done for The Carp-Faced Boy.

I am forever grateful to my brilliant and luminescent agent, Ethan Ellenberg and everyone at the Ethan Ellenberg Literary Agency. Ethan believed in me, and he continues believing in me, and that believing-in-me keeps me going when I'm shaky and not sure about this writing thing. Ethan, I want to make you proud.

Thank you, Julyan Ray Matsuura, son extraordinaire. You are stronger than anyone I know. You teach me more about living and life than I could ever teach you. You're my inspiration. You make it all worthwhile. I thank the Universe that you are my kid. There is no greater gift.

I will never forget and be forever grateful to all of my classmates, instructors, helpers, and supporters at Clarion West 2015. We were eighteen strangers and we became family. There is no escaping. Ever. There I said it. I want to give a special hug to Evan J. Peterson. It was his snippet of autobiography that I was allowed to re-imagine and take full liberties with that became the story, "My Dog Bucky".

I also want to give a kaiju-sized arigatou to those who supported and beta read, boozed and fed me. You are so much more than the head gaffers and key grips. You are the charming and the beautiful. You are my muses. You are the reason I wake up in the morning and the reason I keep trudging on. My Book Clubbers: Joanna Matsunaga, Jennifer Nelson, Steve Redford, Patty Suzuki, and Jean Taylor. Josiah Smith who reads and encourages and says what needs to be said. My Prince(ess) Michelle Shene, whose shoulder I've cried on more than any other. You've always had my back.

There are also my shiny-shiny, tiara-wearing tipplers Pamela Jewell and Leah Strebin. We've got something special. Distance can't keep us apart.

Fist bumps and mega props to these three guys:
Christopher McClory, voracious reader, lover of a great story, your taste is impeccable. You've made me laugh when all I wanted to do was cry. Your stoicism and sage advice continues to keep me afloat. Thank you.

Gabriel Novo, more than the best writing buddy in the world, you're also an outstanding story teller, the keenest of editors, and the bestest of friends. Our lives are strangely simpatico. We've been through our respective hells and back, and we've got so many more stories to tell. You have pulled me from the ledge more times than I can count. Thank you.

Lastly but not leastly, Richard Pavonarius. I'm filled to the top. There is too much to say. The truth is: You're not unharmonious at all. The truth is: You brought me back to life. Thank you.

And thank you to everyone else – you know who you are – who kept me – and continue to keep me – this side of sane.

AVAILABLE BOOKS

BENEATH THE NIGHT
by Greg F. Gifune
Novel & Novella - **Paperback Edition**
October 2016

ALL AMERICAN HORROR OF THE 21st CENTURY
edited by Mort Castle
Anthology - **Paperback Edition**
with stories by Jack Ketchum, Steve Rasnic Tem, Sarah Langan,
David Morrell, Tom Monteleone, F. Paul Wilson, Livia Llewellyn, Paul
Tremblay, and many others
November 2016

THE BEAUTY OF DEATH
Edited by Alessandro Manzetti
with stories by Peter Straub, Ramsey Campbell, John Skipp,
Poppy Z. Brite, Edward Lee, and many others
Anthology - **eBook Edition**
July 2016

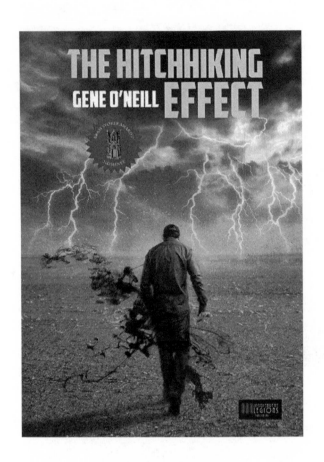

THE HITCHHIKING EFFECT
by Gene O'Neill
Collection - **eBook Edition**
February 2016

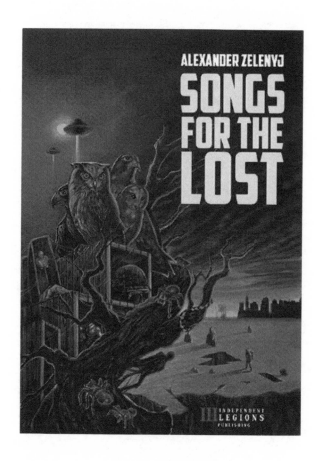

SONGS FOR THE LOST
by Alexander Zelenyj
Collection - **eBook Edition**
April 2016

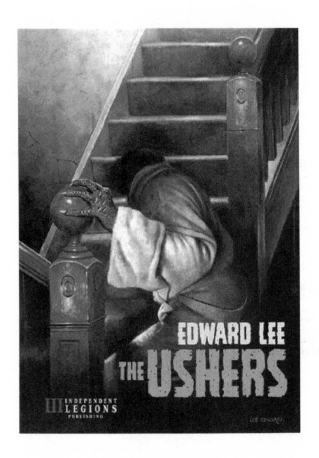

THE USHERS
by Edward Lee
Collection - **eBook Edition**
May 2016

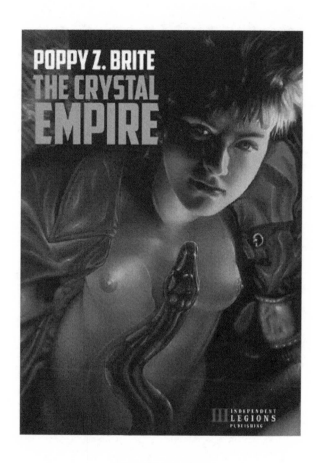

THE CRYSTAL EMPIRE
by Poppy Z. Brite
Novella - **eBook Edition**
May 2016

USED STORIES
by Poppy Z. Brite
Collection - **eBook Edition**
June 2016

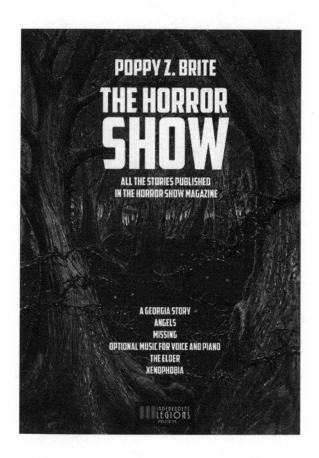

THE HORROR SHOW
by Poppy Z. Brite
Collection - **eBook Edition**
August 2016

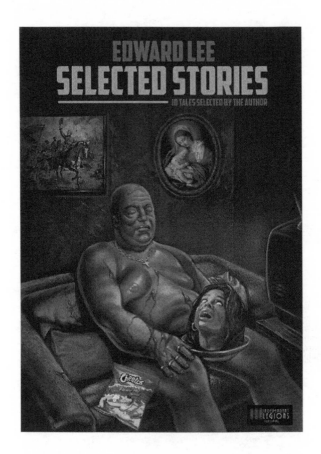

SELECTED STORIES
by Edward Lee
Collection - **eBook Edition**
July 2016

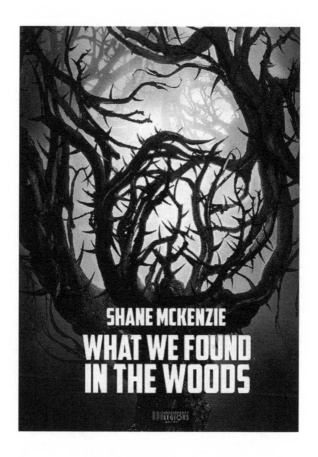

WHAT WE FOUND IN THE WOODS
by Shane McKenzie
Collection - **eBook Edition**
September 2016

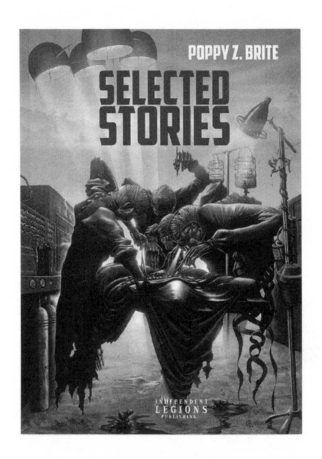

SELECTED STORIES
by Poppy Z. Brite
Collection - **eBook Edition**
February 2016

DOCTOR BRITE
by Poppy Z. Brite
Collection - **eBook Edition**
January 2017

Independent Legions Publishing
by Alessandro Manzetti
Via Castelbianco, 8 - 00168 Roma (Italy)
www.independentlegions.com
www.facebook.com/independentlegions

Made in the USA
Middletown, DE
01 March 2017